As Sophie watched Zach drive out of the parking lot, she suddenly felt overwhelmed.

She wondered what was happening. Dinner with Zach's parents tomorrow night was simply business. They wanted to know about their son's progress. Nothing more.

So, why did she feel so confused? Zach's kiss.

Obviously Zach had feelings for her as proved by what just happened, but where had those feelings sprung from? Gratitude. Simply gratitude for his recovery. Nothing more.

She'd pushed him into riding again, forced him to face the life he'd left. She demanded the best from him and didn't accept excuses.

He'd responded to that tough love with an eagerness that surprised her.

So had he misinterpreted his own feelings?

And what about her feelings? Zach tapped into the attraction she'd felt for him so long ago, but watching him struggle and watching him interact with the kids, she gained a respect for the man. She admired him. That was it. Nothing more.

Too bad that logic didn't feel right.

Books by Leann Harris

Love Inspired

Second Chance Ranch

Love Inspired Suspense

Hidden Deception
Guarded Secrets

LEANN HARRIS

When Leann Harris was first introduced to her husband in college she knew she would never date the man. He was a graduate student getting a PhD in physics, and Leann had purposely taken a second year of biology in high school to avoid taking physics. So much for first impressions. They have been married thirty-eight years and still approach life from very different angles.

After graduating from the University of Texas at Austin, Leann taught math and science to deaf high school students for a couple of years until the birth of her first child. When her youngest child started school, Leann decided to fulfill a lifelong dream and began writing.

She is a founding member and former president of the Dallas Area Romance Writers. Leann lives in Dallas, Texas, with her husband. Visit her at her website, www.leannharris.com.

Second Chance Ranch
Leann Harris

WITHDRAWN

Steeple
Hill®

Published by Steeple Hill Books™

STEEPLE HILL BOOKS

Steeple
Hill®

Recycling programs
for this product may
not exist in your area.

ISBN-13: 978-0-373-87646-4

SECOND CHANCE RANCH

Copyright © 2011 by Barbara M. Harrison

www.SteepleHill.com

Printed in U.S.A.

I pray also that the eyes of your heart may be
enlightened in order that you may know
the hope to which He has called you…
—*Ephesians* 1:18

To the men and women of the U.S. Military, all current and former members. Thank you for your service to this country.

Acknowledgments

I want to thank:

Brenda Rozinsky and Ariane Mele at Equest Therapeutic Horsemanship Ranch for their help.

Donald R. Cummings at Scottish Rite Hospital in Dallas for his generous time and explaining to me how prosthesis limbs work.

Theresa Zumwalt and Jane Graves for your insight with horses.

Chapter One

Zachary McClure closed his eyes and breathed in the calming and familiar smells of the barn—horses, grains, leather and liniment. He hadn't smelled anything that comforting in the past four years. Dust, diesel and fear had filled his days in Iraq. Disinfectant, moans and sickness had filled his last year in the hospital. The smell of horses took him back to pre-army days. That was before—

He stopped the thought. He couldn't change the past.

"You all right?"

Zach opened his eyes and looked into his sister's concerned face. Beth had always looked up to him, but lately they argued a lot. He hadn't wanted to come today, didn't want to face the ghosts of his past and the limitations of today, but she kept badgering him with phone calls and coming by his apartment, telling him he needed to start riding again. He tried sending her home, but somehow she got him to agree to come once here to the New Hope Ranch.

"I am."

"C'mon. My friend Sophie is waiting for us." Beth linked her arm with his and started moving forward. "You remember her? She was my roommate in college."

He definitely remembered Sophie Powell. The weekend Beth brought Sophie home he'd been thunderstruck by the coltish girl. She wasn't model-beautiful, but there'd been a beauty about her. It had been her eyes, piercing blue. And her smile set him back on his heels. She had a crooked nose with freckles scattered across it and her cheeks. But that only added to her beauty. "I remember," he muttered. *Only too well,* he silently added.

Beth leaned close and whispered, "I think she had a crush on you."

"What?" Zach's head jerked around and his gaze clashed with Beth's. Her grin told him she was teasing him. Yet, there was a twinkle in her eye that made him wonder *if* maybe it was true.

"And she's ex-army, too."

This had the smell of a setup.

They walked down through the walkway between the stable and the office. Children's voices filled the air with laughter and excitement.

When they emerged, he could see the two practice rings. In the far ring a horse with its rider and two spotters moved around the enclosure. On the far side of the rings stood bleachers where three people sat, watching. In front of the closest ring, a woman knelt before a horse. A young boy, maybe six or seven, stood beside her.

"Will he bite?" the boy asked, eyeing the reddish-brown horse.

"No, *she* won't. You should give it a try. Samantha, or as we call her, Sam, is very gentle."

Zach remembered that low, rich voice. Sophie's. He often wondered what had become of his sister's college roommate and had wanted to ask, but that would've given his sis ideas.

Sophie held an apple in her hand. "Put your hand out," she instructed, "and I'll give you the apple."

The boy frowned at Sophie, then at the apple.

"You sure? I saw the b-i-g teeth." The boy kept his hand clenched in a fist.

Zach felt a smile bubble up, but he knew Sophie wouldn't appreciate his reaction.

She nodded. "I'm sure. Sam's my friend. She can be your friend, too."

The boy glanced around and saw Zach and Beth.

Without thinking, Zach walked over to the pair and took the apple from Sophie's hand. Her startled gaze locked with his. The connection was instantaneous and well remembered. Silently, he asked her permission.

Her nod was almost imperceptible.

Zach hooked his cane over his left forearm and put the apple into his right hand.

"You need to make sure your hand is flat. It makes it easier for the horse to get the apple if your fingers are not in the way," he explained. "I'm sure Sam wouldn't want to bite your fingers, so you have to make it easy for her."

The boy's eyes widened.

Zach showed the boy how to hold the apple, then offered it to the horse. Sam opened her mouth and took the apple.

"Wow. Can I try?"

"Sure." He looked at Sophie.

She stood and walked over to the barrel by one of the wooden porch columns, opened it and pulled out another apple. She gave it to Zach.

"Open your hand," Zach instructed the boy. When he looked up, doubt colored the youngster's eyes.

"Would you like for me to help?"

He nodded his head. "'Kay."

Zach moved behind the boy. Zach wished he could've squatted, but the prosthesis wouldn't allow it. Instead he put the apple in the boy's outstretched hand. "Now, be sure your fingers are out straight."

Zach slipped his big hand under the boy's and they moved their hands to the horse's mouth. Sam's lips and teeth picked up the apple.

The boy giggled. "That tickles."

Sam chewed happily.

Zach grinned.

Sophie's eyes twinkled. The lady's impact on him hadn't diminished over the years.

She stepped to their side. "Would you like to ride Sam?" she asked the boy.

"Okay." He turned to Zach. "My name is Andy. I come here to ride. Mom says riding's goin' to help me. Is that so? What if I fall off the horse?"

He was way over his head here. Zach glanced at Sophie, hoping for some sort of direction.

"You don't have to worry about falling, Andy. You see all the other people around here walking beside the riders? That's to make sure no one falls."

Andy looked around. "Oh." He turned to Zach. "Are you here to help me? Will you walk beside me?"

The question took Zach by surprise.

"This is Zach's first time here," Sophie explained. She stood on the other side of Andy. "He doesn't know how to be a sidewalker."

A mulish frown settled on Andy's face, and he crossed his arms over his chest. He looked at Zach. "Would you ride with me?"

Zach swallowed. "Well, Andy, I haven't been riding in a few years. Besides, my leg doesn't work as well as it used to."

Andy looked at Zach's legs, then at the cane hanging over Zach's arm. "Why?"

Suddenly the air filled with tension. He glanced at his sister, then Sophie. Did they think he'd go off on the kid? Zach leaned close and whispered, "I have a fake foot and calf."

"Calf?" Andy frowned.

Nodding, Zach pulled up his pant leg and showed the prosthesis on his right leg to Andy.

"That's cool. Can I touch it?"

"Maybe—" Sophie started.

"Sure."

The boy squatted and touched the artificial leg. His eyes widened. "Wow. How'd that happen?"

Sophie stepped in. "You want to ride, Andy?"

"Can Zach help? He can walk beside me."

"Sophie knows how this works. I don't." Zach turned to her. "What do you want me to do?"

The tension seeped out of her shoulders. "I'll lead Sam and you can walk on one side of Sam, and Beth on the other. Will that work for you, Andy?"

"Yes," he crowed, hopping to his feet. He patted Zach's arm. "It's okay about your leg. I've got Down's."

"Really?"

Andy nodded. "Mom says I'm extraspecial."

"She's right."

Sophie smiled at Zach. "Thanks," she mouthed.

Satisfaction spread through Zach's chest.

They walked to the mounting steps. Sophie got the horse into position. Andy scrambled up the steps.

"Put on your helmet, Andy," Sophie called out.

He raced back down the steps and over to the row of helmets sitting on a shelf at the end of the stalls. He grabbed a helmet and put it on. He raced back to the steps. Zach rested his cane against the side of the stable by the mounting steps.

"Let Zach help you get on the horse, Andy," Sophie instructed.

Whoa, he didn't know how he was to help. Glancing at his sister, he silently questioned her.

"Just support him as he slips his leg over the pad," she instructed, "then guide his foot into the stirrup."

Resting his hands around Andy's waist, Zach lifted the boy onto the saddle blanket. A smile curved Andy's mouth.

Beth helped Andy put his leg in the stirrup attached to the blanket.

"Now, just hold his leg to make sure he doesn't slip," Beth instructed her brother. Beth had been here before and worked as a sidewalker.

"What do you say, Andy?" Sophie asked from her place by Sam's head.

"Go forward," Andy crowed.

Sam started walking.

Zach grabbed the front of the saddle pad and his other hand rested on Andy's leg. Andy turned and smiled at Zach. His heart overturned. With the warm New Mexico sun on his back and the feel of the horse under his hand, Zach felt a peace in his soul—a peace he hadn't felt in a long, long time.

Oddly enough, Zach, Beth and Sophie worked in tandem, he on the left side of the horse, Beth on the right, and Sophie leading Sam.

After three times around the ring, Zach felt the strain in his arms and legs. He stumbled, and his artificial leg folded underneath him, and he fell to the ground.

Andy cried out in dismay. Beth raced to Zach's side. Sophie started to move away from Sam, but Zach waved her back.

"I'm okay."

All the activity in both rings stopped. One of the sidewalkers from the next ring came to Zach's side. The man stopped and said, "How do you want to handle this?"

He would've rather faced a terrorist in the streets of Baghdad, instead of being facedown in the dirt in front of his sister and the woman he'd been attracted to. He rolled to his side and told the man how to help him stand. It was slow and awkward as he struggled to his feet. When he stood, Andy clapped.

"You need any more help?" the man asked Zach.

Zach shook his head. He limped over to a bench under the stable's awning, which sheltered the entrance to the stables. He'd been thrown by plenty of wild broncos and bulls in his rodeo days, but there'd been no shame in it. This time, he'd fallen flat on his face walking.

Walking.

What kind of man can't walk?

He closed his eyes and rested his head against one of the porch posts. He knew that coming here this morning was a mistake. He just didn't know how big a mistake it would be.

Sophie looked at Zach. Her heart had skipped a beat earlier when she glanced up and saw him standing above her. Beth had called Sophie at the beginning of this week begging for help with Zach. Beth and Sophie had kept in contact since their college days when they roomed together and Sophie was more than happy to offer her friend a helping hand.

Zachary McClure still took her breath away. Tall, with wide shoulders and narrow hips, he cast a large shadow. Somehow, that handsome face seemed to have aged more than the few years since she'd last seen him. The weariness in his deep blue eyes matched the new lines bracketing his eyes and mouth.

"Is Zach feeling okay?" Andy asked, snapping her out of her memories.

Turning to Andy, Sophie saw the frown crossing his young face. "I think he's fine." She prayed he was.

For the next few minutes Sophie walked Sam, but Andy remained quiet. When she guided Sam toward the steps, she motioned for another sidewalker to help Andy dismount. The instant Andy's feet touched ground he raced to Zach's side.

"I'm sorry you fell," Andy whispered, tears in his voice.

Sophie's heart contracted.

Zach opened his eyes. Sophie felt Beth stop behind her. They both waited breathlessly for Zach's answer.

Reaching out, he ruffled the boy's hair. "I'm okay. Only my pride was damaged."

Andy nodded and moved closer. "I hate it when I trip and the other kids laugh." His lower lip trembled.

Zach slid his arm around Andy's shoulders and pulled him to his side. "I do, too. Makes me feel bad."

Andy nodded. "That's why my mom wanted me to come to ride on the horse. She said it would help me." He touched his stomach. "She said it would make my tummy stronger. Maybe it would help you, too."

Zach's brow arched and he glanced at Sophie as if accusing her of planning that little scene. He couldn't believe that, could he?

"Thanks, buddy."

The boy accepted the praise and leaned against Zach. "Will you be here next time I ride?" The youthful hope in Andy's expression pulled at Sophie's heart.

Zach rubbed his neck. "Well—"

She knelt by Andy's side. "Zach isn't trained for this. He only came today to see what we do here."

Andy faced Zach. "I'm learning. So can you."

Well, Andy certainly didn't beat around the bush.

Andy's mother walked up to the group. "Did you enjoy your ride?" After two sessions when Andy hadn't left his mother's side, she agreed to disappear until the session was over.

"I rode Sam," Andy explained, throwing out his chest. "And I met a new friend, Zach. He's got a fake leg. But he helped me get on Sam. You want to show my mom your funny foot and leg?"

Andy's mother's face lost all color. "I'm—"

Zach stood and smiled at the woman. "I'm glad I could help Andy."

"I asked him to help me again next time, but he told me no." Andy crossed his arms over his chest and stuck out his bottom lip.

Things were quickly getting out of control.

"Andy, Zach needs some practice himself," Sophie gently explained. "Why don't you come back next time and we'll see what we can work out."

Andy glared at the group. "I'd want Zach to help."

Andy's mother stepped in. "We need to get going. Why don't you put up your helmet?" She unbuckled the strap and Andy ran to put his helmet on the rack.

"Thank you," Andy's mother said. After shaking everyone's hand, she led her son down the breezeway to the parking lot behind the stable.

Zach sat back down and closed his eyes.

Sophie faced Beth. Before Sophie could say anything, Beth shook her head.

Sophie knew brother and sister needed time to themselves. She turned and headed toward Sam, who'd been left tied to the ring by the mounting steps and needed to be unsaddled.

Tears gathered in Sophie's eyes as she walked Sam back to her stall. She knew the battle that raged inside Zach. She'd seen that clash countless times in each of the men she treated in Iraq as a medic. She helped soldiers, airmen and civilians survive their wounds. Now she wanted to help those brave men and women win the heart-and-soul skirmish to gain back their lives.

She stopped and pulled off the saddle blanket, resting it on the half wall of the stall.

"I want to save as many as I can," she whispered into Sam's neck. And maybe, just maybe, she could atone for the one life she couldn't save.

Zach sat in the tack room. The humiliation this afternoon hadn't been any worse than when he fell off his horse at his parents' ranch in full view of his family and all the ranch hands. It was the first time he'd been on a horse since before the attack. He'd tried to ride away from the stable and his mount spooked and he fell off. Unfortunately, his prosthesis didn't come out of the stirrup and he'd been dragged around in front of the stable. When his brother, Ethan, caught the horse, he hit the release button, breaking the vacuum holding the prosthesis onto Zach's leg. His mother had cried, rushing to his side, and his father yelled for his brother to get the horse out of his sight. This afternoon wasn't that gut-wrenching, but had left a mighty bad taste in his mouth. Literally as well as figuratively.

The door to the tack room opened and an old man walked in. He nodded.

Zach acknowledged the greeting with his own nod.

The old guy went about putting up tack. "I saw you ride at the Frontier Days Rodeo in Ocate. It was a great win."

Zach remembered that rodeo held in the little town in northeastern New Mexico. It had been his first all-around championship. He'd been a senior in high school and full of himself. "Thanks."

"You've got a natural talent, Zach McClure."

"Had."

The old guy stopped. "I didn't know talent was in your foot."

The unexpected comeback stunned Zach. The old guy had a point. A smile curved Zach's lips. "I didn't know it, either."

The man walked over to where Zach sat. "When I was young and riding the circuit, I had more drive than sense. I got tossed off a bull. He was a nasty piece of work. Once he throwed me, he came back to stomp on my arm." He shook his head. "I never saw a clown move so fast as to get that bull's attention on him.

"It took me six months to heal. It took another six months for me to get my body back into shape. I kept falling off those mean critters until I built my body back up. I figure with you being in the hospital a while, you got the same problem." He started toward the door.

"You might cut yourself some slack, son." He continued toward the door.

"You know my name. What's yours?" Zach called out.

"Ollie Morton. I'm foreman here."

"Thanks." Zach closed his eyes and shook his head. Was he feeling so sorry for himself that he couldn't see the obvious?

"Did Ollie hit it on the head, Lord?" Zach asked when Ollie had left. As he thought about the foreman's advice, Zach realized he may not have been thrown by a bull, but he might've stumbled onto the truth.

Sophie walked back from stabling Brownie, the small chestnut mare they used with the younger children.

Other riders were exiting the arena and the chatter of happy voices surrounded her. There would be no other lessons today and all the horses needed to be unsaddled, watered and fed.

There were two other hands to help with the horses, but they needed more help. Sophie's boss, Margaret, couldn't help anymore since her stroke six weeks ago, and Margaret's children wanted nothing to do with the facility.

Sophie worked for twenty minutes, putting the horses in the corral on the east side of the barn. Each of their stalls needed to be mucked out, and fresh water, feed and hay put in each one. The large metal building had two main halls that ran parallel. Stalls were on either side of the hall and an enclosed tack room stood at the far western end of the building closest to one set of large double doors. At the end of each hall was another set of double doors leading to the outside corrals.

She tried not to think, but went on automatic with the chores. She prayed under her breath, asking the Lord for wisdom and to comfort Zach's heart.

"Sophie, I've finished. So has Marty," David Somers called out. "You want me to put the horses back in their stalls?"

"No, go on. I'll see to it."

He nodded and disappeared.

Each of the horses had earned an extra treat and praise for their performance today. She wished Ollie was still here, but with her encouragement he'd gone to the hospital to see Margaret.

Sophie put new hay in Sam's stall and walked to the tack room to put up the lead ropes she used. Sitting on a bale of hay was Zach. In his hands he held one of the bridles. Those strong hands worked over the leather, cleaning it.

Sophie stopped and stared at him. "You're still here?"

"I am."

Now what? Zachary McClure had a way of rattling her that no other man had. She had no trouble dealing with the soldiers in her unit or her patients. None of them had this effect on her of making her stomach flip-flop. She tried to ignore the feeling.

Zach's hands stilled. "I've been thinking a lot about what happened this afternoon."

He hadn't been the only one. She'd played the scene over and over in her mind, wondering what she could've done differently. She knew that Beth had worked weeks to get Zach here, and then to have him trip in the middle of the ring… She wanted to run over to him and help him up, but she knew he wouldn't appreciate it. He'd been rodeoing since he was in middle school and had been on track for a championship rodeo buckle before he joined the army.

"This afternoon with Andy has been the best afternoon I've had in a long time." He closed his eyes, and a satisfied smile curved his mouth. "I wanted to get up on Sam myself and ride." His wistful smile nearly brought her to her knees. "It's a dream for me."

Sophie held her breath. There was hope here.

He opened his eyes and his gaze met hers. "Beth told me you wanted to start a program for wounded soldiers."

"That's true. One of the guys I treated when I was a medic in Baghdad was a double amputee, losing both his arms. But when I saw him riding at the stables near Walter Reed with such joy on his face, I knew what I wanted to do." There'd been a certainty in her heart she knew God had given her. "I knew Margaret had started a therapy group here. She and I talked about expanding the program to include vets, also. We wanted to approach the army to see if they would use our program for their wounded vets."

He nodded and went back to working the cloth over the bridle.

There was more she wanted to say to him, she knew, but she didn't know how to bridge that gap. "Want to help me bring in the horses for the night? Ollie's off visiting Margaret, the ranch owner who's in the hospital, and the rest of my help has left."

His head came up and she read hunger in his eyes. "Yeah, I'll help." He hung the bridle on a hook beside the other tack, placed the rag in the bin below and grabbed his cane.

As he walked to the door, Sophie saw flickers of the old Zach she knew. Her nerves danced with excitement and hope.

"Lead the way, Miss Sophie Powell."

"That's Lieutenant Powell."

"I outrank you. I was a captain."

"A smart officer listens to his subordinates who know more than he does." The instant the words left her mouth, she wanted to snatch them back.

His mouth curved into a smile. "You're right. A smart officer listens to his men."

"And you're going to listen to me?"

He nodded. "You're the expert."

"Smart move."

"Finally, after months of knocking my head against the wall." The corner of his mouth tilted up.

She knew about knocking one's head against the wall. She'd been an expert at that.

The day had cooled and the sweet smell of pine filled the air as they walked in silence to the corral behind the barn. Sophie's heart soared with hope—the hope Zach wanted to ride.

"How long have you been working here?" Zach asked.

"I mustered out nearly twenty months ago. I started riding here in high school." She didn't mention she'd wanted to feel closer to her brother, who died in a riding accident. "In college, I came whenever I was home. I knew Margaret had started working with Down's children when her first grandbaby was born with Down's." She rested her arms on the top rail of the fence. Too bad that daughter had moved to Oregon, leaving her brother and sister here who opposed using the ranch to help children with disabilities. "She and I talked about my dream of seeing if we could help the wounded vets. But just as we were going to present it to the army, she had a stroke."

Sam trotted to the fence and nudged Sophie's hand. She laughed and stroked the white blaze on her nose. "Oh, you're so spoiled."

The horse turned her head toward Zach, nudging his hand. He obliged Sam and patted her neck. "I felt like a fool out there today, eatin' dirt."

Sophie didn't respond.

"I know Beth's been after me for a while to start riding again." He continued to stroke Sam's neck. "She was right. I miss the horses. I miss the physical activities." He turned, facing her. "I'm not in good physical condition, which I've found out the hard way. But maybe I can be your first test case to show the army what equine therapy can do?"

Not sure she heard correctly, she turned toward him. "Really? You want to be my test case?"

"I do."

His words floored her.

"I also want to help around the stable, too. Maybe I could be a sidewalker for some of the kids you deal with."

"I know Andy would love that."

Zach grinned. "Yeah, you're right. He's a persistent little boy."

Here was the dream she had for the future, of helping vets overcome the physical wounds of war. Zachary McClure, ex–rodeo champ and army veteran, wanted to be her first client.

"You sure this is what you want to do?"

He nodded, a grin creasing his mouth. "I spent the afternoon wrestling with my pride, which took a beating. I also questioned God. He and I talked, and it's what I want to do."

"All right. Let's do this."

Chapter Two

After they finished putting the horses in their stalls, they walked to the stable's office.

"When would you like to start?" Sophie asked, collapsing into her chair.

He settled in the chair beside the desk. "Work me around the other therapy sessions."

"How about tomorrow morning?"

Zach leaned back in his chair and laughed. "You're not going to let me chicken out, are you?"

Sophie felt the heat in her cheeks as she blushed. "That's what the army taught me. You get permission, you act."

"How long were you in theater?"

His question caught her by surprise. "I did a full tour there, plus my tour was extended twice. I was all over Iraq, but mostly around Baghdad and Fallujah."

He nodded. "Summer's a killer."

"You want to start tomorrow?" she pressed, refusing to be diverted.

"Fine. Tomorrow it is. What time?"

She glanced at the schedule. "8:00 a.m. We'll do it before any other appointments."

He studied her. "I'll be here."

Her tension melted away.

"You need a ride home?" Sophie asked going to the door.

"I'll just call for a taxi."

She shook her head. "No. I'll drive you home."

He opened his mouth, then closed it, stood and joined her at the door. "So you had a crush on me in college," he said, his voice full of mirth.

Sophie's hand froze on the key in the office door. Zach leaned his shoulder against the building, his body filling her vision. He arched his brow as he waited.

"Wh-what are you talking about?"

He lifted one shoulder. "The last thing Beth whispered in my ear before we emerged from the breezeway earlier today was that you had a crush on me while you were in college."

She was going to kill Beth. "I think maybe your sister tried to appeal to your masculine ego. If you knew that I found you attractive, you might be more willing to—"

"You think I'm handsome?"

He wanted to provoke her. She pulled the key from the door. "I'm going to plead the Fifth."

His satisfied grin told her that he understood she hadn't answered the question. He fell into step beside her.

One car stood in the parking lot. Hers. As they approached it, a truck pulled up in front of them.

Zach laughed. "My sister called in the cavalry."

"She called the army?" Sophie asked, totally con-fused.

"No. She called my brother, Ethan."

Ethan was Zach's older brother. When they were in college, Beth told her about the adventures of her two older brothers. They had tolerated a younger sister until she turned thirteen and started attracting male attention. Much to Beth's chagrin, her brothers decided to be her guardians and ran off more boys than Beth could count. It wasn't until she was at the University of New Mexico campus in Albuquerque that she had her first serious boyfriend.

The truck door opened and Ethan got out and came around the front of the truck. "Hey, bro, Beth sent me to pick you up. She said you were kinda prickly." Ethan grinned, wagging his brows. Sophie choked on a cough.

"So she chickened out, did she?" Zach remarked.

Ethan laughed. "No one said Bethie was stupid. A royal pain, yes, but she knows how to save her own skin."

A smile spread across Zach's face and he shook his head. "I assume you agree with her that I needed to get off my backside and start living again."

Ethan crossed his arms and leaned back against the front fender. "Couldn't have said it better myself."

The strong family resemblance between the brothers made one look twice. Ethan and Zach could've been twins. Zach was an inch or so shorter than his brother, and his eyes were blue while Ethan's were gray. But both men were handsome, with dark hair, strong cheeks and full mouths. Ethan grinned easily. Zach didn't.

Apparently, Beth wasn't the only McClure sibling who wanted to help Zach. Interesting.

"Well, I'm glad that you feel that way. I'm going to have my first session tomorrow morning at eight."

Ethan jerked up straight. "Really?"

"That's right, and I'll need someone to help in the session, won't I?" Zach directed the last question at Sophie.

"Huh, yes." Zach's question surprised her, but if he wanted his brother to be the sidewalker, she'd welcome the help. "Since both of you are horse people, I think that Ethan should do fine. I'll have another sidewalker here, but I'd love to have Ethan work with us."

Without any hesitation, Ethan answered, "I'll do whatever you need me to do."

"Then it's set."

"I'll see you all tomorrow."

It took a few moments for Zach to maneuver himself into the passenger side of the truck. He jerked the door closed, rolled the window down and rested his arm on it. "I'll see you tomorrow, Sophie."

"Be prepared to work, Zach."

"I'll be ready."

Alleluia, there was hope. "See you tomorrow."

She stood watching the truck disappear down the road.

Lord, I see the open door and I'll walk through it, but could it have been with someone else? Someone else who hadn't captured my heart and left it in jail.

* * *

"Have I been that much of a pain?" Zach asked his brother.

"Well, let me put it this way. I've been tempted to punch you. My prayer life has certainly increased, little brother."

Zach knew his brother was at the end of his rope. He got called "little brother" only when he was in major trouble.

"I've been that much of a jerk?"

Ethan glanced at him. "Yeah."

This afternoon had torn away the apathy Zach had wrapped himself in. When he woke in Walter Reed Army Hospital and looked at what was left of his leg, he wanted to shout and throw things. He'd reached for the bedpan, but the guy in the next bed stopped him.

"Go ahead and throw it. It won't change anything."

When Zach looked over at the guy, he was minus both of his legs and his left hand and forearm.

After that warning from Bill Jensen, the two men became fast friends. Bill's wife and family had adopted him, and when Zach's mom came to D.C., she considered Bill another son.

There had been so many times after a therapy session when he'd question God about why this happened. Why him? What had he done? The night he read in the Book of Luke about Jesus's death on the cross, he realized that there was nothing He did to deserve such an awful death. What was his loss compared to Jesus's?

Zach had slowly worked through most of his anger. Bill had gone back to his job, teaching in a community college in Wichita Falls, Texas. But what was Zach going to do? Before, he'd planned on following the rodeo circuit, trying to earn a championship belt buckle.

"Today, being with the horses gave me hope. I want to ride again."

"About time."

"So you're ready to come with me each time I ride?" Zach asked.

"I am, and I'll spring for breakfast."

"I really must've been a pain if you're willing to pay for breakfast."

"And then some."

Sophie walked back to the guest cabin. She moved there after Margaret had her stroke. Margaret's son, Austin, had asked her to stay on the property while his mother recuperated. He wanted Sophie to take over the day-to-day running of the ranch since none of Margaret's kids wanted to divide their time between their jobs and their mother's ranch.

Austin complained about having to continue with the equine-therapy sessions, but several of the parents had bought package sessions for their children, and Austin didn't want to refund the money. The ranch foreman, Ollie Morton, had planned to retire at the end of the month but he agreed to stay until Margaret could hire a replacement.

Sophie let herself into the cabin. No welcoming aromas from a cooked dinner filled the air. The hum of the refrigerator cut off, leaving the house silent. Sophie loved being with the horses, but she needed a maid. Or someone to take care of the mundane things like fixing dinner and washing her clothes. In the army, she had three square meals a day and clean clothes.

She pulled a frozen dinner out of the freezer compartment and popped it into the microwave. What had the women a hundred years ago done after a long day of working on the farm? The phone rang the same instant the microwave dinged. She picked up the wall phone. "Hello."

"You're a miracle worker, Sophie," Beth gushed.

"I wish."

"You don't know how hard I had to argue with Zach this morning. I had almost given up when I told him that his heart wanted to be back on a horse. And then I prayed under my breath." She laughed. "I'm surprised I didn't have a wreck on the way to the stable. Every time I stopped at a light, I closed my eyes and prayed."

"Well, your prayers were answered."

"Oh, Sophie, I thought it was all over when Zach tripped. I wanted to die."

"I'm glad you were strong, Beth. He had to face the truth that he needs to rebuild his strength."

"You're right. I tell you the first time I saw him without his foot and on crutches, I wanted to break down and cry."

"He needs you to treat him as you always have—like a pain-in-the-neck big brother. He's the same man."

Beth remained quiet.

"He needs that consistency. He needs to know that the essence of the man Zach was is still there, and his family still sees the old Zach."

Sophie thought she'd gone too far, but she heard Beth sigh. "You're right. And he's coming tomorrow to ride."

Sophie heard the tears clogging Beth's throat.

"This afternoon when I walked into the tack room and saw him, I didn't know what to think. I know some demons were defeated in that room today."

"Mom and Dad are excited and want to come and help."

News in the McClure family traveled fast. She wished it were the same in her family. Her mother hadn't talked to her grandmother in over fifteen years, and they both lived in the same little town of twenty-four hundred people. "Let's give him a few times before he has an audience, okay? I don't know how things are going to go tomorrow, and I think if Zach doesn't have an audience, it will be easier."

"I hadn't thought about it. I'll call them."

"I do have a bone to pick with you, friend."

"Oh?"

"Why did you tell Zach I had a crush on him in college?" When he'd thrown that out at her, Sophie didn't know how to answer. Sure she'd been attracted to the handsome cowboy. His loose-hipped walk and cocky grin appealed to anyone with two X chromosomes. And she fell into that category.

"Hmm, I thought it would ease him into the situation. It certainly gave him something to think about besides his discomfort."

It had done that. "I think we have Andy to thank for our success. And your prayers."

"Will you let me know how the session goes tomorrow?" Beth asked.

"You're not coming with Zach?"

"No. I'll let Ethan do it instead of me. He'll be more help than I could be."

"Okay. I'll give you a call."

After hanging up, Sophie took her dinner out of the microwave. Settling at the kitchen table, she pulled her Bible toward her and opened it up to the book of Psalms. The twenty-third Psalm was her favorite. *The Lord is my shepherd, I shall not want.*

In high school, her best friend's family were shepherds. She'd had some wonderful insight as to how the author of the Psalm felt. Her friend explained how they were responsible to move the sheep from one pasture to the next where there was abundant grass. The sheep didn't move until the shepherd led them to another place.

"Okay, Lord, You've led me here. Help tomorrow to meet Zach's needs."

At seven the next morning Sophie walked out to the stable, heading for the office.

"Want some coffee?" she called out to Ollie who was inspecting all the horses' tack.

"Sure. Bring it black, none of that fancy stuff," Ollie answered.

"Fancy stuff?"

"Cream and sugar."

"And do you eat your steak still mooing?" she retorted.

"Is there any other way?"

Sophie grinned. She walked into the office and poured two mugs of coffee. Ollie always started a pot of coffee when he arrived at the ranch. She opened the mini-fridge, pulled out her favorite French vanilla creamer and poured it in her mug. When she carried the mugs outside and gave Ollie his coffee, he glanced at the brown coffee in her mug and shook his head.

"Sissy."

She shrugged her shoulder. Looking out over the rings, and hearing the morning sounds, Sophie knew this was where she belonged.

"You're going to miss this when you retire, Ollie." She took a sip of her coffee.

"Nope. I'm going to sleep in until seven and get up and spend hours reading the newspaper."

"Fibber."

He simply grinned.

"Will you help me this morning with the rider who's coming?"

"Sure. Who's comin'?"

"Zach McClure."

"Ah, the guy with the fake foot."

She winced. Ollie didn't pull any punches, but there was not a mean bone in his body. "He was a wonderful rider. Watching him ride…" She could still remember how awed she'd been watching him practice calf roping. "It's like he was born on a horse." She heard the wistfulness in her voice.

Ollie's mug stopped inches from his mouth.

Sophie realized her feelings colored her comments.

"Zach's sister was my roommate in college," she hurried to explain. "I went home with her several times. She was with him yesterday."

Ollie took a swallow of his coffee. "I saw him when he was a teenager. He had a talent."

"Really?"

"Best I'd seen up 'til that time."

Then Ollie would understand. "He lost his foot when a roadside bomb caught his patrol in Baghdad." She looked down into her coffee. "I think that talent awoke yesterday. He's willing to work to get stronger."

Ollie nodded. "My son was in the First Gulf War. He needed help when he came home. I'll do it."

Those were the most words that Ollie had spoken since she knew him. And she never knew he had a son. Maybe Zach's rehab would touch more than Zach himself.

She heard a car pull into the parking lot. It was seven-thirty.

"Looks like your client is here," he murmured, looking down at his watch. "And I think he's eager."

She prayed Ollie was right.

Chapter Three

Ethan pulled the key out of the ignition. "You ready to do this?"

Zach had tossed and turned all night and finally gave up trying to sleep at five this morning. He spent the time praying and reading his Bible. For the first time in a long time he felt like himself. "I am."

They got out of the truck and walked toward the office. Some of the horses were in a corral on the other side of the stable.

"There's some good-looking horse flesh out there," Ethan commented.

From what Zach saw he had to agree with his brother. "I'll have to ask where they get their stock."

They emerged from the tunnel and saw Sophie and Ollie resting up against the hitching rail. The sun kissed Sophie's skin and her brown hair danced with red tones in the sunlight. The braided tresses nearly came to her waist. She'd been beautiful at eighteen, but now there was a maturity about this woman. That coltish girl had become a stunning woman.

"Good morning," Ethan called out, touching the brim of his cowboy hat.

"Good to see you this morning," Sophie replied, pushing off the rail. She introduced Ollie.

"We've met," Zach said, meeting Ollie's gaze.

Sophie looked from Zach to Ollie. Apparently the old guy hadn't told Sophie of their little chat. His opinion of the ranch foreman went up.

"You ready?"

"I am. And Ethan's up for the session."

"He couldn't keep me away," Ethan added.

Zach didn't know whether to be encouraged by his big brother's eagerness or insulted.

"Let me go get Prince Charming, and we'll start." Sophie put her mug on the apple barrel and turned to Ollie. "You want to go get the tack?"

Ethan straightened up, then glanced at his brother. He grinned. "Prince Charming?"

Ollie nodded. "He's the right size for a man of Zach's stature—sixteen hands." He nodded at Sophie. "She calls him Prince Charming." He shook his head. "What kind of name…" He headed for the tack room.

A whirlwind of feeling churned in Zach's stomach. He lifted his hat and wiped the sweat off his forehead. He wanted to ride so much he could taste it. He watched as Sophie pulled a halter out of one of the stalls, grabbed a lead rope and carrot from the pail on a bench in front of the stalls and walked to the corral beside the stable.

At the gate, she called out. A handsome black horse with a star on his nose and his left hind foot with a "white stocking" trotted up to her. She crooned to the magnificent gelding and offered the carrot.

The man in Zach reacted to her tender treatment of the horse. He glanced at his brother and saw Ethan smiling at him.

As Prince Charming ate the carrot, Sophie rubbed his nose. When he finished the carrot, he nudged her hand. "No, I don't have another one. It's time to work, big boy."

The horse nodded and allowed Sophie to put the halter over his head and attach the lead rope. She opened the gate and led him to where Zach stood.

Ollie quickly put the saddle blanket and pad on Prince Charming's back. He handed Ethan one of the stirrups to attach to the pad.

"No saddle?" Ethan asked.

She shook her head. "I've been in constant contact with the folks running the rehab program outside of D.C. For the first few times, we want to have Zach ride without the saddle. It will exercise his muscles."

Doubt colored Zach's eyes. "I could've jumped up on his back in my rodeo days, but now—"

"That's why you should try the mounting block. You're going to be asking your body to do a lot of work today, Zach, which it hasn't done in a while. You've got to focus on the final goal."

His pride fought with his common sense. *Lord, this is hard to swallow.*

His gaze touched each person's face. He saw only support, but in Sophie's eyes, he saw something else. A promise. He reached out and stroked the horse's nose. "You going to be nice to a rusty cowpoke?"

Prince Charming nudged his hand. Zach patted the horse's neck. "I'll take that as a yes."

Taking a deep breath, Zach walked up the steps of the mounting block. Ollie and Ethan took their positions on either side of the horse. Zach handed his cane to Ethan, put his foot into the left-side stirrup, then threw his right leg over the horse's back. He tried a couple of times to get his prosthesis into the stirrup attached to the saddle blanket. Ollie helped. He pushed back his cowboy hat and a spark of admiration lit his eyes.

Using the mounting block wasn't as big a deal as Zach had thought it might be. He looked down into Sophie's face. She smiled. "You look good."

He felt good. The world lay at his feet. "Let's move."

"You want a helmet, Zach?" she asked. "It's just a precaution."

He was willing to go just so far. "I'm okay."

She didn't try to argue but led Prince Charming into the arena. She walked around the perimeter of the ring.

"Things look much better up here," Zach commented.

"Amen, brother," Ethan quietly said. A hint of moisture gathered in his eyes.

They walked around the arena for close to thirty minutes. Zach realized the muscles of his stomach and thighs were protesting.

"How are you feeling?" Sophie asked, looking over her shoulder.

He didn't want to admit weakness. "I'm okay."

She accepted his word and they worked for another ten minutes before she called a halt to the session. She led the horse toward the mounting block.

"I won't need that," Zach told her.

"Zach," Sophie said, touching his leg, "I don't recommend that."

"I can dismount by myself." *Pride cometh before a fall.* The verse ran through his head.

She looked to Ethan for help.

"Uh, maybe she's right, Zach."

There was no saddle horn for him to grab on to to keep his balance and he felt a cramp in his injured right leg. There were a lot of scars up and down that leg.

"Okay." The word tasted bitter in his mouth.

She walked the horse to the mounting block. Zach pushed up on his left leg and swung his right leg over the horse's rump. When his prosthesis hit the wood, it folded on him. He tumbled back off the horse. Ethan stepped up and caught him. His left foot remained in the stirrup. Prince Charming didn't dance or spook. He stood calmly. Ollie sprinted around the horse and disengaged Zach's foot.

Ethan pulled Zach backward so his feet could touch the ground. His right leg didn't hold. Ethan's arms clamped around Zach's chest, holding him upright. Zach's hat fell to the ground.

Zach struggled to make his right leg work. Quietly, Sophie handed him his cane. He grabbed the lifeline and used the cane for balance. After struggling for a moment, he found his balance. Ethan picked up Zach's hat.

"We probably worked too long," Sophie said.

Zach wanted to rail that Andy had more endurance than he did. He nodded. "Ethan, you want to drive me home?"

Sophie dropped the horse's leads. "Zach—"

He shook his head and started to walk away.

Prince Charming turned his head and caught Zach's attention. The horse bobbed his head.

"He's expecting a carrot," Ollie offered. He nodded toward a pail on the bench. Zach took two steps and looked inside. Carrots. He pulled one out and turned toward the horse. Prince Charming readily accepted the treat.

Sophie stood on the other side of Prince Charming, gently rubbing his neck, her eyes dark with worry. He didn't—couldn't—acknowledge her.

With a final pat on Prince Charming's shoulder, Zach turned and walked toward the parking lot.

What made him think that he could be the man he used to be?

Sophie buried her face in Prince Charming's neck, taking comfort from the strength and smell of the horse.

"Give him a few minutes."

Her head jerked up and she found Ethan standing beside her. "We never scheduled another lesson," she said.

"I'll talk to him." Sadness and concern creased Ethan's face. "Seeing him on a horse was great. I'll have him call you to set up another appointment."

She nodded and watched as Ethan walked toward the parking lot.

"Lord, touch his heart," she whispered.

"Don't you worry, Miss Sophie. I saw a spark in that young man's eyes. Once he wrestles his pride down, you'll see him again."

She glanced over Prince Charming's neck to Ollie. "I pray you're right."

Over the next week, Sophie held on to Ollie's words. She heard nothing from Zach. She called Beth, asking about Zach.

"He's not taking my calls," Beth informed her. "If I was in town, I'd drive out to his apartment and face him down again." Beth did a lot of traveling for her job with a big department store headquartered in Santa Fe. "I told Ethan to talk to him, but I haven't heard back from him."

Sophie couldn't wait any longer. Andy's next session was scheduled for tomorrow. "Give me your brother's address."

Beth gave her the street number of the new and trendy condominium and town house.

Sophie helped Ollie finish putting out feed for all the horses. She stopped by Prince Charming's stall.

"Hello, handsome."

The big horse stuck his head out of the top half of the door. He nudged her hand.

"You are so spoiled," she said, rubbing his nose. "I'm

going to try to get Zach. You were great with him. Now he needs to understand that he needs you."

Prince Charming nodded.

"You like him? He's a real cowboy. Well, I like him, too. I'll see what I can do to bring him back."

Driving to Zach's place, she prayed for wisdom and the right words to touch the stubborn man.

The new complex of town houses stood on the eastern edge of the city, built at the foot of one of the mountains surrounding the city. She found the number of his town house and parked. She whispered the opening lines of the twenty-third Psalm as she exited her car and walked up to the door and knocked.

Nothing.

She knocked again. "Zach, it's Sophie."

After several more seconds, the door opened. He was unshaved, and his closed expression didn't give her any hope.

"I was hoping to talk to you."

He studied her. "Why?"

Well, at least he didn't shut the door in her face. "I wanted to talk about your next lesson."

He shrugged his shoulders and walked back into the living room.

She followed him, closing the door gently behind her.

"How have you been doing?"

He shrugged again, settling into a leather recliner in front of a sixty-inch plasma TV. A baseball game flickered on the screen.

She walked to the sofa. "I think we pushed your first time too far. We should've stopped earlier."

He didn't respond.

"Zach, talk to me."

He turned to her and nailed her with his blazing gaze. "What do you want me to say? Yeah, I didn't tell you the truth when you asked if I was tired. I'm less of a man now than I was when I blew you off when Beth came home during college."

It was a reaction, but not the one she hoped for. "What I see is a man who's trying to come back. What I see is a man who helped a young boy overcome his fear and enjoy his ride on a horse."

He turned away from her, staring down at the head of his cane.

"Zach, the man I met in college was full of himself and knew his strengths. One of those strengths was a faith in God and a determination to do the right thing." She pulled a pamphlet out of her purse and put it on the coffee table. "This is from NARHA."

He gave her a puzzled frown.

"North American Riding for the Handicapped Association. It talks about equine therapy and its benefits. What you expected from your body was unreasonable."

His head came up and he looked at the pamphlet.

"When I fought for the guys who were wounded on the battlefield, I wanted to save them all. The ones who survived were blessings. You have a duty to those who didn't make it. You lost a foot, but I don't think you lost your soul. The Zach McClure I knew is still inside you. You just have a challenge you've never faced before."

She stood. "Andy's session is tomorrow morning at ten. He's told all his friends about you, and I've had two more mothers of Down's children call me, wanting to start with equine therapy." She started for the door. Pausing with her hand on the knob, she turned to him. "I will never leave a fallen comrade." With those final words she walked out the door.

I will never leave a fallen comrade. The words of the U.S. Military's Honor Ethos echoed in Zach's brain. How many times had he gone back to get a fellow wounded soldier. With the guys who were gravely wounded, their survival depended on their individual will to live.

He'd made it. The roadside bomb that wounded him had killed two members of his team. He didn't remember much after the bomb, except his good buddy calling for him to hold on and telling him that they'd get him help.

They kept him sedated until he woke up in Walter Reed Army Hospital.

He picked up his Bible and turned to Exodus. The story that always amazed him was Joshua's. This was a man who led Israel after Moses's death in their fight to conquer the Promised Land.

Zach turned over to the book of Joshua and read the first three chapters, where Joshua faced his first major obstacle—the Jordan River. Not just a normal river but a river ten times its usual size. That crossing was a major miracle.

He faced his own Jordan River.

God gave Joshua a plan, and if Zach didn't miss his guess, God just gave him a plan. And it started with showing up to help Andy.

Chapter Four

Zach took a deep breath and glanced at his brother, who sat behind the steering wheel of his truck. Zach chaffed at having to be driven, but he didn't want his truck fitted with hand controls. He wanted to be able to build up the strength in his leg to be able to drive his own truck.

"You sure you don't want me to stay?" Ethan asked.

Ethan had quickly covered up his surprise this morning when Zach called, asking for a ride.

"I'm sure."

Ethan studied him. "I'll stop by after I finish the business at the bank."

Zach put on his straw hat. It was already warm beyond normal for an early spring morning. "I'm okay, Ethan." He clamped his hand on his brother's shoulder. "Thanks."

Ethan nodded.

Zach opened the truck door and carefully rested his feet on the ground. He used his cane for balance.

Hopefully, he could permanently retire it in a few weeks with hard work and exercise.

He walked down the breezeway to the open rings. The first thing Zach saw was Andy. The boy sat on a bench by the helmets. He stared at the ground. Glancing up, he spotted Zach.

"You came," Andy yelled, launching himself off the bench.

Zach braced himself for Andy's hug. The boy stopped and looked up at Zach. He reached out and grasped the boy's hand. Andy snuggled close to Zach's side.

"I see your sidewalker is here."

Zach's head snapped up. Sophie stood before him, her blue eyes glistened with moisture, and he read approval and something else there. But before he could analyze it, Andy raced toward Sam.

"Hi, Sam." Andy stroked the horse's shoulder.

Sam turned her head toward the boy.

Pride for Andy's actions filled Zach. The boy overcame his fear. It was something Zach needed to do.

"Get your helmet, and I'll take Sam to the mounting ramp," Sophie instructed.

Andy dashed off.

A smile curved Sophie's mouth. "I'm glad you're here. Andy was disappointed when he didn't see you."

"What did you tell him?" He waited, curious for the answer.

"I told him that Sam was glad he was here."

"Is that all?" He moved toward her and lightly ran his hand over Sam's withers.

She held his gaze. "When he asked about you, I told

him that things would be okay. I prayed. I know Andy is happy you're here and…"

Zach understood the unspoken part of her sentence. She was glad he was here, too.

"I got my helmet," Andy yelled, waving it above his head.

"We're coming," Sophie replied.

Suddenly Zach knew that his "Jordon" could be divided.

Andy cheerfully waved one last time at Zach as his mother pulled him down the walkway. "I had fun. I'll see you next time."

Another child called out Sophie's name as she rounded the corner. "Miss Sophie. I'm here." The little girl's braids bounced as she waved.

"Go put your things in the office." Each rider had a small cubbyhole on the inside wall of the office for their things. "I need to take Sam back to his stall." Sophie lightly patted the horse's withers.

Zach grasped Sam's leads. "I'll take care of Sam."

She hesitated. "You sure? I didn't expect you to work."

"I'm sure. I've been doing this kind of thing since I could walk." He paused. "I think before I could walk. I remember my mother talked about taking me out to the barn and something about a pen." That sounded bad to his ears.

She laughed.

"Take care of your other clients. I'll take care of Sam."

Her eyes danced with mirth and the corner of her mouth kicked up. "You've got a deal."

Satisfaction raced through him. As he watched Sophie walk toward her next client, Zach's heart lightened. He was where he belonged. Sophie somehow touched his heart in a way he didn't understand.

Sam nudged his arm.

"What? You want a carrot, or are you thinkin' the same thing I am?" Zach rubbed Sam's nose. The horse lipped his hand.

"A carrot is what you want?" Zach walked to the barrel where the treats were kept and pulled out a carrot. Sam took the offered treat. Zach glanced at his cane propped in the corner behind the mounting steps and decided he felt strong enough to leave it there.

Over the next hour, Zach plunged into the wonderful pattern of caring for a horse. After removing Sam's tack, he walked the horse down to the shower stall and hosed him off. Even this early in the spring, the day would be a scorcher and Sam deserved a cooling shower.

Sam also ate up the attention. She was a flirt.

"I see you found the shower," Ollie said, walking by.

"Sam worked hard and I thought she'd like a little refreshing."

Ollie pushed the straw hat back on his forehead. "I'm glad to see you here."

Ollie's words surprised him. "I couldn't disappoint Andy."

"You need a sidewalker, count me in."

Ollie's offer touched Zach.

"Thanks."

"No thanks necessary. It's my privilege." He nodded and walked down the row of stalls.

Shock and amazement held Zach motionless. Ollie obviously was a man of few words, but each one held power. Ollie believed in him, which humbled Zach.

Untying Sam's lead, he said, "C'mon, girl, let's go."

Sophie grabbed an apple out of the mini-fridge and walked out of the ranch office. There'd been no time to eat and this would be her lunch. Things had happened so quickly this morning that it reminded her of the mornings in the field hospital in Iraq when she went on autopilot.

Finally, things had settled down and no clients were scheduled for the next hour and she could think. She'd panicked when Andy and his mother had shown up and there was no Zach. Her heart soared when Zach walked out of the breezeway.

Where was he now? She moved down the row of stalls and found him outside, looking at the horses in the corral.

"I was worried that you might have disappeared."

He turned to her and flashed a wide smile. "No, I haven't left."

She noted a hint of satisfaction in his voice. "You were great with Andy."

He took off his hat and ran his fingers through his hair. "I couldn't have disappointed him, but I'll admit I was nervous when I got here today."

He didn't know how much prayer went into today.

"It did go well. Andy didn't tire as easily as he did last time. You didn't, either."

"You're right. My leg held up nicely. Of course I took my time with Sam. She didn't mind if I sat down and caught my breath." He shook his head. "It was a one-sided talk, but Sam didn't mind."

"So, you ready to ride a little today?"

He glanced around. "You've got time today?"

"We have an hour, and I have Ollie and another volunteer to be sidewalkers if you're willing."

He nodded. "Let's do it."

"If you want to get Prince Charming, I'll get his tack and meet you at the mounting steps."

Zach walked to Prince Charming's stall while Sophie grabbed the tack and blanket and walked to the mounting steps.

Ollie and Ethan stood with Zach. Zach held Prince Charming by his halter.

"I see we have a new sidewalker," Sophie greeted as she walked to the group.

Ollie took the tack, and Sophie threw the blanket over Prince Charming's back. Quickly they got the horse ready for the ride. This time when Zach mounted the horse, things went smoothly.

Sophie led Prince Charming into the ring. She stopped and glanced over her shoulder at Zach. "When you're ready, tell Prince Charming."

He nodded. She could see the excitement in Zach's face.

Zach patted Prince Charming's shoulder. "Let's go."

Prince Charming started forward.

After their first time around the ring, Zach asked, "Why'd you name him Prince Charming?"

Ollie snorted.

"What's that mean?" Ethan asked.

"'Cause this guy was an unruly beast when we first got him."

"So how'd he get the name Prince Charming?" Zach asked.

Sophie shrugged, but didn't turn around. "Because he reminded me of the horse in the storybook I read as a girl. I thought there was a wonderful horse under all that bad behavior. I was right. I worked with him and earned his trust. Prince Charming is only used with adult patients." She glanced over at Ethan. "We all have our bad moments. The place where Margaret got Prince Charming was a ranch in southern Colorado. Something happened. I think the owner was some city dude and didn't know much about horses."

They worked for close to twenty minutes, making rounds of the corral.

"Let me know when you're tired."

"I think a couple more times around, then we can call a halt to it."

Both Ollie and Ethan nodded in approval.

With a final round of the corral, Sophie guided Prince Charming to the mounting stairs. She held her breath as Zach swung his prosthesis over Prince Charming's back. His artificial foot rested on the platform.

She held her breath and Ethan tensed, ready to dart forward and help his brother.

Zach continued to hold on to the saddle blanket and

slipped his good leg out of the stirrup. He paused for a moment, getting his balance. Slowly he released the saddle blanket and stood.

Tears welled in Sophie's eyes. Zach took a step back, turned and smiled at her.

"I listened to my body this time."

"That's good." She forced the words around the lump in her throat.

He held on to the railing as he walked down the stairs. Prince Charming nodded his head, as if agreeing with Sophie.

"I think this guy needs a carrot."

Sophie grabbed a carrot and gave it to Zach. Prince Charming took the offered treat.

Zach's stomach rumbled. Prince Charming nudged Zach with his nose.

"I guess I'm hungry, too."

Ollie took the leads from Sophie. "I'll take care of Prince Charming while you folks get something to eat."

"If you got time, I'll take us to the burger stand down the road," Ethan said.

Sophie glanced at her watch. "Can you get me back in forty minutes?"

"I can."

When Sophie hesitated, Zach added, "Trust me when I say if Ethan said it, we can do it."

Zach words sounded as if they came from experience. She should turn them down, but the success of the morning needed to be celebrated.

"Let's go."

* * *

They squeezed Sophie between Zach and Ethan. Zach rested his cane between his legs. The morning had gone better than anything he could've hoped for. Zach wanted to grin, feeling young and more like himself than he had in forever. *Thank You, Lord,* he thought.

"So how'd my little brother do this morning?" Ethan asked.

Sophie turned to Zach. "He did great. He made Andy's day."

The truck rattled down the dirt road. When the front passenger wheel hit a hole, Sophie was thrown against Zach. Before they could do anything, she bounced away.

Zach's mind registered that although Sophie worked hard, she was still a feminine woman.

And he a man.

He felt the pull of attraction to her. She stole a glance at him. Her cheeks flushed pink.

Would she be attracted to him as a man? He knew she wanted to help him and he volunteered to be her test case for the army, but did it go beyond that?

The balance of the eight-minute trip passed in silence. Zach didn't see the mountains in the distance or the small stream that ran alongside the road. Trees grew on the other side of the bank, but didn't stop the glare of the sun off the river. As the road curved around the hill, a building came into view. Freddie's Burgers and Fries was painted on the sign beside the restaurant. Beyond the restaurant was a gas station and mini-mart.

Ethan pulled the truck into the parking lot of the restaurant. They climbed out of the truck, and walked inside and placed their orders. The crowd had begun to thin and they found a table in the corner of the dining room.

"I guess the food in here's good." Ethan looked around at the cowboys and high school students.

A teenage boy brought the tray of burgers and onion rings to the table.

Both Zach and Ethan reached for the onion rings. The taste of batter and onion exploded on Zach's tongue. "Try the onion rings," he encouraged Sophie.

"I think I'm in love," Ethan said after he swallowed his bite.

She laughed at the brothers. "Beth said you guys were a challenge."

"What?" Ethan grabbed another onion ring.

"I heard how you two bullied every boy that came near Beth." She pulled an onion ring from the plastic basket and took a bite.

Zach shook his head. "Beth had terrible taste in boyfriends." He shrugged. "We couldn't leave her defenseless."

Sophie snagged another onion ring. "That's not exactly how Beth tells it."

Both men laughed.

"Oh, I don't doubt that," Ethan replied. "She probably described us as Attila the Hun and his horde."

"That's not exactly how she described it."

As they ate their hamburgers, stories from Beth's

dating flowed around the table. The more they talked, Zach noticed a longing that entered Sophie's eyes. More than once, she covered up by laughing at something he or Ethan said.

At the end of the meal, one onion ring remained in the basket. "Why don't you have that last onion ring, Sophie?"

She raised her hands. "They're good, but I'm full. Besides, I don't want any of the horses to pass out from my breath."

They piled back into the truck and drove back to the ranch.

"How are you feeling now, Zach?" Sophie asked.

His energy level seemed to be coming back, especially after the meal. "I'm good."

She nodded her approval.

The morning had gone smoothly. What was even better was that Sophie hadn't made a big deal out of his showing up. She acted as if she expected him to be there and he appreciated her attitude. "When do you think we can do another session?" he asked.

"I'd give your body a day's rest. We could try Friday." Her smile took some of the sting out of the words. "If you push too hard now, before your body's ready, we'll lose ground."

He didn't like the reality of it, but he knew Sophie was right. It had taken a couple of days for him to recover from his first session where he overdid things. "Okay."

They agreed to a Friday-morning ride before everyone else's appointment.

"I think Beth would like to help," Ethan informed them.

Zach shrugged.

The ranch parking lot came into view. Although he wanted to stay the afternoon, he knew that wisdom demanded he go home.

Ethan drove his truck to the entrance.

Zach opened the door and got out of the truck. Sophie followed.

She turned to him and he could see she was ready to argue.

"I'll see you O-eight-hundred on Friday."

The stiffness went out of her spine. He knew his words shocked her.

"I want to ride again, Sophie, but I know common sense when I hear it."

"You're an unusual man, Zach McClure."

"Why do you say that?" he asked.

"Because you're letting common sense rule over ego."

"No. I'm just a man who finally has a goal—to ride again. I don't need Prince Charming to scold me like Balaam's donkey scolded him."

She frowned.

"You remember that story in the Old Testament— Numbers, I believe, where the Balaam was asked to curse the children of Israel and his donkey avoided the avenging angel standing in the road?"

She studied him. "I do, but you wouldn't have beaten Prince Charming."

"True, but he would've sensed my weakness."

"Good thinking." She laughed and disappeared around the corner of the stables.

Zach slipped back into the truck.

"What were you two whispering about?" Ethan asked as they drove off.

"Sophie thinks I've got more sense than a donkey."

Ethan frowned. "What does that mean?"

Zach laughed.

Sophie walked into the ranch office and checked the afternoon schedule. The answering machine blinked. She hit the button to listen to the messages. Two of the messages were from new clients wanting information about riding lessons for their children.

The last message was from Beth who wanted to talk.

Sophie called.

"Did he show up?" Beth asked breathlessly. "I called his house, but he didn't answer his phone. And he doesn't own a cell phone anymore. He threw it away when he moved to that apartment."

"He did? Why?"

"Because he didn't want to have to talk to us, and if he didn't have the cell phone, he couldn't answer our questions when he was out. He said it made him feel like a dog with a microchip."

"Everything's good, Beth. He showed up and helped with Andy." She explained how Zach had worked this morning, then rode again. "He stopped when he was tired."

"My prayers have been answered."

"Well, you need to keep praying. It's the first step and it's going to be a long road."

"It's a start, Sophie. I—" A quiet sob stopped her. "He's coming on Friday morning for another lesson."

"Oh, Sophie, I'm out of town. I'm scheduled to go to New York on a buying trip for the store."

"Ollie will be here to help."

"Can I call Mom and Dad and tell them the good news? They are dying to know what's happening."

"Sure. Of course, if Ethan talked, it will be old news."

"Ethan's so tight-lipped, he wouldn't tell me if the house burned down. I'll call." She laughed. "You know, Sophie, I think you can handle Zach in a way none of the rest of us can."

"I'm not family. It's easier for a stranger to tell him the truth than his family. He knows I'm not trying to spare his feelings."

"Maybe. But I think it's more than that. Zach looks at you—"

"What are you talking about?"

"There's something more. I don't know how to describe it. I'll tell you this, I haven't seen that look in his eyes with any other girl."

Obviously her friend was giddy with excitement and didn't know what she was talking about. Sophie shook it off.

"I'll call you when I get back into town," Beth said.

The dial tone sounded in Sophie's ear. She pulled the handset away from her ear and stared at it.

Beth hung up on her. Hung up.

Sophie put the phone back. What on earth was Beth trying to imply? Zach looked at her in a different way. And that "way" was boredom. Indifference. She was his sister's bothersome roommate.

"Miss Sophie, we're here," Penny Littledeer called out.

"I'm coming," Sophie called back as she raced out of the office, Beth's words ringing in her ears.

Chapter Five

Ethan's cell rang. He pulled it out of his shirt pocket and offered it to Zach. "Answer it. I'm driving."

Zach looked at the ID. Beth.

"I think you should talk to Beth." Zach tried to hand the phone back.

"No, no. You answer it."

Zach could let it go to voice mail, but it would only postpone the inquisition.

"Hello."

"Zach? Are you with Ethan?"

"I am. He's driving me home." He waited for his sister's reply. "I'll put you on speaker." He hit the button to allow Ethan to hear, too.

"Aren't you going to tell me about this morning?"

"What do you want to know?" Zach wouldn't make this easy for her.

"Stop stalling. How was your ride? Are you okay?"

He laughed and told her how the morning went.

"He did great," Ethan added.

The joy in Beth's voice told him of her delight and

relief. Glancing at Ethan, he saw his brother's involvement in the conversation. It hit him then that both of his siblings had suffered with him as he struggled to find himself again. The realization of how selfish he'd been hit him hard. "My next lesson is Friday morning."

"I won't be there. I'll be in New York."

"Don't worry about it. Someone has to work." After they said their goodbyes, he hung up and handed the phone to Ethan.

Putting the phone back in his shirt pocket, Ethan laughed. "I'm amazed how our sis knows everything the instant it happens."

"It is one of the mysteries of the universe." It had been that way ever since Beth had turned thirteen. He and Ethan might have turned into guard dogs, but Beth returned the favor by monitoring their movements as teenage boys.

"Do you remember when Beth dragged Sophie home?" Ethan asked as he negotiated the truck onto the interstate.

Zach remembered. He'd come in from checking fences, wet and grumpy, and found his sister and her roommate in the kitchen giggling. Beth threw her arms around him, kissed him, then introduced Sophie. She stood by the refrigerator and looked like she'd been touched by the angels with the sun streaming through the windows causing red highlights to dance in her hair.

"Yeah, I remember that weekend. My horse stepped into a gopher hole and I had to walk miles to the barn in my new boots."

"And if I remember, you were wet."

"That was because Clancey was spooked by the isolated thunderstorm that broke over our head." A more sure-footed horse Zach had never had, so that accident had rattled him. There hadn't been another place to seek shelter on that stretch of desert where it rained.

"You had some bad luck that weekend."

There'd been all sorts of reasons why he'd been on the wrong side of annoyed. Aside from the fact it had rained on his new boots, he'd also managed to put a gash in the leather. But when he clapped eyes on Sophie, something in him shifted, tipping him off balance. There was a certain fragileness in her that hit him in the heart. It wasn't her frame or build, but there was something in her eyes that spoke of a longing.

And need.

But what shook him was his reaction to her. He wanted to wrap his arms around her and ask her why she looked so lonely, but sanity quickly returned and he knew he had to keep his distance. Ethan had been stupid enough to date one of Beth's friends. After two dates, things went south and Ethan didn't hear the end of it for a year after that. Ethan made sure Zach was as miserable as Beth made him.

Yet, when Zach decided he didn't want to act on his feelings, he regretted it.

"What I remember is you stomped around like a bull with a cocklebur in his hide that weekend and nothing made you happy."

"I ruined my new boots."

Ethan's laughter filled the cab. Zach shook his head, but he had to smile looking back at it. He hadn't handled things well that weekend. Added to the chaos was his reaction to Sophie.

Later that night as Zach got ready for bed, his thoughts continued to swirl around Sophie. He sat on the side of the bed and took off his artificial leg, placing it by the nightstand. His crutches leaned against the nightstand.

He took off the protective stocking that cushioned the end of his leg. In the hospital in D.C., seeing other patients, both male and female without their limb wasn't uncommon. It didn't shock him anymore, but the first time his mother saw his leg, her eyes filled with tears.

What would Sophie think? Would her reaction show her distaste and revulsion? Or would she cry like his mother? There'd been countless times in the hospital when family members would visit their loved ones and see them without their artificial limbs. The two main reactions to seeing the stumps were revulsion or pity. Neither reaction appealed to him.

He stretched out on the bed, picked up the remote and turned off the bedside lamp. Rolling to his side, he let his thoughts return to Sophie.

His conversation with Ethan brought up so many memories. After that first weekend when Sophie and Beth came home from college, he'd seen Sophie a couple of times after that. Once when he visited Beth at school, he'd offered to take both girls to dinner, but Sophie declined, claiming to have a test to study for.

After he'd graduated from college and been commissioned as an officer in the army, he went to UNM to say goodbye to Beth. There'd been a moment when he and Sophie had been waiting for his sister. Sophie had asked why he'd joined the army. He'd told her that both his father and grandfather had been in the army. It was a family tradition. What he hadn't mentioned was that the only way he could afford school was with the army's help. Those were lean years for the ranch.

His last trip to see Beth was when they attended her college graduation. Sophie hadn't been there. Beth told the family that Sophie had signed up for the army and she'd already gone to basic training.

At that news, a small flare of hope settled in Zach's chest. Maybe their paths could cross? If a person was stationed in Baghdad, the chances of running into old friends weren't good, but it did happen.

They hadn't met. Instead, he ended up going home early wounded. He couldn't stop wondering what her reaction would be if she saw him without his artificial leg? She'd been a medic and had seen worse things. She'd already proven that pity wasn't in her vocabulary.

He folded his hands behind his head. Sophie Powell was a lady with guts. And smarts.

It was something he admired. And was attracted to.

Sophie's stomach knotted. Doubts about whether or not Zach would show up plagued her. He said he'd come, but she worked with vets who said they wanted help, wanted to ride, but ended up not showing. She walked to Sam's stall. The horse came to the door and stuck her head out.

"Hello, you sweet thing." Sophie rubbed Sam's nose. "You ready to work today?"

"I am."

Sophie whirled and faced Zach.

Zach stepped to Sophie's side and lightly stroked the horse on her neck. "Sorry I startled you. I'm not late for Andy's ride, am I?"

"He only comes on Mondays and Wednesdays. But you can help me with a new student who signed up last week."

"A newbie like me."

"You can see how we start. This little girl had a stroke and her mom feels riding will help."

"Really?"

"You've been riding for years and didn't know how beneficial it was?"

His hand stopped stroking Sam's neck. "There's a lot of things I've forgotten. But I'm ready to relearn those things. And I believe I'll see them in a new light." He shook his head. "Who would've thought that mucking out a stable could hold such appeal for me?"

"And hope."

"Really?"

"Absolutely." The word rang down the aisle of stalls.

"If you're willing to work, I'm happy to have the help. Right now, I want you to take Sam to the mounting steps while I get the tack. Later I can show you some of the specialized tack we use."

"I'll meet you there."

"Good to have you on the team, Zach."

He paused, as if he savored the word. "Teamwork, huh?"

"That's it. Teamwork. And sometimes our path with a rider isn't a straight line. We might take two steps forward and one back. But we keep going."

He didn't say anything, but he needed to understand if he started this therapy it wasn't going to be easy or a straight shot, but he would improve.

"Teamwork it is."

She could breathe again and smiled at him. When he grinned back at her, suddenly her mind short-circuited and butterflies filled her stomach.

After several moments, Zach said, "Your new student is looking at us."

His words snapped her out of her stupor and she turned and raced away.

An hour later, Zach led Sam to her stall. Thoughts of a little girl sitting atop Sam, smiling and enjoying herself, filled his head.

"Sam, I'm impressed what a patient, wonderful lady you are."

The horse nodded.

The little girl fell in love with Sam and was eager to ride. Sophie had gently led Sam around the ring, talking to the little girl. It had been obvious when the rider tired and Sophie had ended the session. There'd be nothing but praise for the child.

"Your performance was great, Sam," Zach whispered

to the horse as he put her into the stall. He went to work caring for the mare, talking to her, telling her what a good horse she was.

The morning passed quickly and Zach helped Sophie with two more riders. At noon, he walked into the office, needing a few moments to rest. His leg throbbed and he knew he couldn't go any farther. His cane rested in the corner of the office, but he was to the point where he didn't need it unless he was extremely tired. Pride led him to be stupid the last time. This time, he'd listen to his body.

Ollie motioned Zach to the back of the room to the table and chairs. "Sit yourself down, and rest a minute."

Zach joined the older man.

"You've been a great help this morning," Ollie said.

"There's a lot of work here."

Ollie rubbed his neck. "Yeah, since Margaret had her stroke, work's kinda built up." He stood up and poured himself a cup of coffee. "Want some?"

"Yes."

"I hope you like it black, because I don't do that fancy stuff that Sophie does."

"In the army you drink it black."

"A man after my own heart." He poured a second cup and brought it to the table.

Zach sipped the dark brew.

Ollie studied him. "You going to be hanging around here for a while?"

"Plan to. I want to work with Sophie to get a program

for vets going." He needed to ask Sophie who'd she contacted at the army. He might have more connections she could use.

"Good. Sophie needs to have some help. Margaret's not in any shape to do it."

Zach took another gulp of his coffee, sensing Ollie had more to say, and the old cowpoke would take his time at getting there.

Ollie leaned back in his chair and took another gulp of his coffee. "We're going to need some more help here at the ranch."

"I see volunteers working."

"Yup." Ollie ran his hand over his face. "But what we need is someone who knows his way around horses, who can direct things when Sophie is tied up. Make no mistake, we can't do it without the volunteers, but I'd feel better with someone who knows his way around stock. You know horses and been with them a long time. This ranch could use your help."

"Are you going to quit, Ollie? Is that why you're looking for a replacement?"

Ollie leaned forward, nailing Zach with a hard stare. "I was set to quit, but Margaret had her stroke. I told Sophie I'd stay, but I hadn't counted on my doc telling me I've got cancer. I'm going to the hospital next week and get cut on."

"Does Sophie know about this?"

"I haven't told her and don't plan to. She's a strong lady but I ain't going to burden her with my news. But she's going to need someone to help her with her thoughts."

Zach knew Sophie's world was about to crash in on her. "I'm far from being up to speed."

"So? You got a brain and can see what needs to be done. You can tell the volunteers what to do. Guide them. As you build up your strength, you can do things yourself.

"Sophie needs someone here who knows horses. Someone to lean on. I plan to continue, but I heard that those treatments make you puke out your guts. There might be days I'm worthless. I don't want to do that to Sophie. She's working her heart out here. I think maybe if I'm here and you're here, we can keep going."

Questions whirled around in Zach's mind. "Is there any chance that the owner's children or friends might help? Wouldn't they want to keep the ranch going? Or is there someone else who might help? Sophie's family? Your family?"

"Sophie's family?" Ollie snorted. "I don't recall them ever being here or calling. Don't count on them. As for Margaret's kids, forget it. The two that are in town are as worthless as—" He swallowed the rest. "They don't like what Margaret's done. They'd be just as happy if we shut down the program.

"My son lives up in the Northwest. He has a lot on his plate." Ollie shook his head. "The way I see it, I think the good Lord above sent you to help Miss Sophie. And she's the one who can help you."

Zach wasn't sure he'd agree with Ollie's conclusions. Divine intervention?

The door to the office opened and Sophie walked in with three sack lunches. "I hope you two are hungry."

Walking to the table, she held up the sacks. "I've got one turkey sandwich, one bologna and one peanut butter." Placing the sacks on the table, she looked from Zach to Ollie. "Anything wrong?"

"No," Ollie answered. "I'll take the bologna. You got Fritos in there, too?"

"I do. And a chocolate-chip cookie. I didn't bake it, but Andy's mother brought me some the other day." She handed Ollie the sack with the bologna. Turning to Zach, she asked, "Which one?"

"Give me the peanut butter."

Once they all started eating their sandwiches, Sophie looked from one man to the other. "What were you guys talking about?"

Ollie's request shook Zach to his core, and yet it resonated with him as nothing else had since he woke in the hospital. He was needed here. He wasn't up to the mark, but he could help and direct the other volunteers. "I was just talking to Ollie, asking him if he thought I might start coming every day to help around here."

Sophie put her sandwich on the brown paper sack. "Why would you want to do that, Zach?"

He caught Ollie's eye and the old man silently questioned him.

"I thought that I might gain strength quicker if I was here every day, helping a little here and there. Also, I know the owner is in the hospital. I thought you might need another hand who's spent his fair share of time with horses.

"Besides, I'm going stir crazy in my place, looking at

the walls. Being outside can only help me build up my strength. And we can work on your plan for soldiers."

Sophie's eyes widened and she sat back in her chair. The longer she remained quiet the more nervous Zach became.

"You sure you want to do this?" she asked.

He released the pent-up breath. "Yeah. I'm sure."

Her eyes twinkled and a smile curved her mouth that Zach felt all the way to his toes. She held out her hand. "Welcome to the New Hope Ranch, Zachary McClure."

He shook her hand.

Ollie held out his hand. "Welcome, son."

As they walked out of the office after lunch, Ollie stopped Zach.

"Thanks for keeping my secret."

"I think you should tell her about your situation."

"Maybe, in time."

Before Zach could question him further, Ethan showed up. "You ready to ride, little brother?"

"I'm ready," Zach replied. And he knew he was ready for this challenge.

Sophie walked into room 320 of All Saints Hospital, expecting to see Margaret Stillwell. However, the room stood empty. Panic seized her. Sophie hurried to the nurses' desk.

"Where's Margaret Stillwell? Her room's empty."

The nurse looked up from her charts. "They moved her this afternoon to a rehab hospital."

Sophie took a deep breath. *Thank You, Lord.* "What hospital?"

The nurse gave her the address of the rehab hospital. It took Sophie ten minutes to get to the older hospital on the western edge of Albuquerque. Once inside the building, she found Margaret's room after stopping at the front desk.

Margaret lay in the bed, watching TV. The stroke had affected her speech and the left side of her body.

Sophie smiled down at her dear friend. Margaret had become a surrogate mother to her. And Sophie had been like the daughter who was close to her mother, talking daily about the running of the ranch. Margaret's other children didn't fit that bill.

Sophie laced her fingers with Margaret's and sat. "How are you feeling today?"

Margaret turned her head toward Sophie.

"I'll tell you I had quite a scare when I walked into All Saints and found your room empty." A tear slid down Sophie's cheek. "Are you comfortable here, Margaret?"

With her free hand, Sophie finger-combed the gray hair from her friend's face. "I want to tell you of an old friend who's working at the ranch. My ex-roommate's brother lost his right foot when he was in Baghdad. He was a championship rodeo rider, and you know what? He's going to be a great rider again when he builds himself back up. He's had a bad time, Margaret, but you know about that.

"Well, Zach's going to help me with our plans to start the therapy for the wounded vets. He's riding

Prince Charming and helping around the ranch." Sophie thought she saw approval in her friend's eyes.

"I'll admit I'm grateful for his help. And—" Sophie wanted to tell someone of her feelings. "First time I saw him, he was wet, dripping from being caught in a rainstorm, and he was madder than a wet hen. But he took my breath away.

"Of course, he ignored me. I was his little sister's college roommate and off limits." Sophie shrugged. "He's still a hunk." A bark of laughter burst from her lips. "A hunk with an attitude.

"Well, I fell head over heels for him. I felt like a thirteen-year-old with her first crush. He yanked all the right chains." She stroked Margaret's hand. Margaret squeezed back, letting Sophie know she was listening. "Of course, Zach had no interest in me. I could've been part of the wallpaper. But I had all sorts of dreams about him."

A smile settled on Margaret's face.

"I'll tell you all the guys in my unit and the guys I treated would laugh themselves silly if they knew about my crush. I was known as the best medic they had, but don't mess with the lady. She ain't buying."

"What are you doing here?"

Sophie turned and came face-to-face with Austin Stillwell, Margaret's oldest son. "I'm visiting with your mother."

His eyes narrowed. "It's late for you to be visiting."

Looking at the wall clock, Sophie noted the time as seven fifty-five.

"I would've been here earlier, but I went to All Saints

and discovered your mother had been moved here. I thought she might enjoy some conversation."

Austin didn't look any more pleased with her explanation than he did with her presence.

"How does the doctor say she is doing? When do they think she'll be able to come home?"

"The doctor doesn't see her coming home. Her therapy is going to be long and cos—complicated."

He almost said *costly* and Sophie knew that Austin's bottom line was money.

"Surely, she could be at her home and recuperate there?"

Austin straightened his spine as if he was lecturing a child. "We don't know how quickly she'll respond. But I know this—she will be in no condition to continue running the ranch."

"Between Ollie and myself, we have that covered so don't worry about it."

"I think you misunderstood what I said, Miss Powell. The horse-therapy thing needs to come to an end. Mother will not be able to participate in it."

She hadn't misunderstood. Sophie knew exactly what Austin was doing. He never liked having the ranch used for equine therapy. She'd heard him complain several times to his mother about "those kinds of people" using the ranch. Sophie also knew that Austin refused to have anything to do with his nephew who had Down's.

Sophie let go of Margaret's hand and stood. "I don't think Margaret would want the therapy program shut down."

"That's your interpretation of my mother's wishes. Mine is to shut it down."

This couldn't be happening. The kids who came to New Hope were making great strides. And more came daily. And what about her plans for the vets?

Tamping down the panic, her mind raced to think of a way to stop Austin.

"Well, I must warn you, if you shut things down, you will have to repay several of the parents for the therapy."

The little bombshell she tossed rocked Austin back on his heels.

"What are you talking about?"

"I'm saying that nearly half the parents of kids we having coming have paid for lessons through the end of May." Eight weeks. That's how long the ranch was obligated to run sessions.

She could see Austin calculating how much money he'd have to pay back.

"I'll talk it over with the lawyers and the others. I'll get back to you. But in the meantime, don't take on any more clients."

"We've just had three new inquiries about riding lessons. And you know your mother and I wanted the army to use the ranch for therapy for wounded soldiers."

His mouth tightened.

There was a noise from the bed. Sophie and Austin looked down at Margaret. She blinked and her mouth twitched.

"What is it, Margaret?" Sophie asked.

The older woman's gaze settled on her son.

"What, Mom? You want this army thing to go through?"

Margaret blinked twice.

"I think she's answering you, Austin."

"You're just hoping, Ms. Powell."

"No." Sophie turned to Margaret. "Blink once for no and twice for yes. This is your son, Austin."

Margaret blinked twice.

"Could be a twitch."

"And I'm Sophia Loren."

Margaret gave a single blink.

"Don't I wish," Sophie said under her breath. "I'm Sophie Powell, one of your workers at the ranch."

Margaret acknowledged her.

"You see there. Your mom wants me to continue."

"Finish out the contracts."

Sophie knew that she'd pushed Austin into a corner. She only prayed that she could get that army contract, then Austin might change his tune.

Leaning down, Sophie kissed Margaret's cheek. "Get well, friend. Things are going well. Don't worry. And I'll be praying for you."

As Sophie left the room, she stopped by Austin's side. "I think your mother will recover quicker if she knows her dream is well and helping kids. She also wanted the contract with the army. And if you don't believe me, check her office. Our proposal is there."

If looks could kill, Austin would've ended her life there in the hospital room.

As she drove home, Sophie sent up a silent prayer of thanks that they put their plans for the ranch in writing.

They'd also put into writing that if at any time Margaret wanted to sell the ranch, Sophie had the first right to buy. When Margaret first suggested it, Sophie thought Margaret was ridiculous. Now, she knew Margaret had been following her heart, guided by a Higher Power.

Chapter Six

Sophie paused as she entered the last figure into the spreadsheet for payments received for lessons. Their balance sheet looked good, and Austin couldn't complain about the bottom line.

But he would. She hadn't heard from him since that night at the hospital two weeks ago, but she'd felt the pressure.

She rubbed the back of her neck to ease the tension. *I know, Lord, I need to trust in Your plans. I'm trying, but—*

Her world had been turned on its head.

Zach had shown up every day and worked around the ranch, keeping her off balance and fighting her feelings. Zach helped with caring for the horses and by acting as a sidewalker. He slowly built up his strength during his time at the ranch.

Sophie immediately felt the difference that Zach's presence made. She didn't have to cover everything or worry that the volunteers might not know what to do. Oddly enough, Ollie had called in sick and had been gone half a week. Zach filled that gap. Both Beth and Ethan also showed up and helped, filling in and doing Ollie's chores. And since they'd grown up with horses, they were a blessing.

When Ollie returned the next Monday, he moved slowly and Sophie worried about her friend's health. Zach took up the slack.

Zach smiled often and Sophie felt her heart opening up to him. But when she caught herself hoping for more, she remembered one of the shrinks at Walter Reed had warned her not to become personally involved with patients because too many people misread gratitude for love. She'd watched doomed relationships with therapists and patients. And she'd made that mistake, too, misinterpreting gratitude for something deeper.

So here she was again, her heart leading her. Could she trust it? And what of Zach? When he smiled and gave her that killer grin of his, was there more to it than just pleasure that he was now gaining his life back? Or gratitude for someone helping him?

Added to the mix, she'd had four more parents call, asking to bring their children to the ranch for therapy.

"You look puzzled." Zach's voice broke into her thoughts.

She looked up from the desk in the office and saw him in the doorway. He looked more and more like his old self. He smiled more readily these days.

"I was thinking about Ollie. I'm worried about him. He doesn't seem up to speed. There are days he looks fine and other days—" She shook her head.

Last week, she'd rounded the stables and caught him throwing up.

Zach settled in the chair by the side of the desk.

"Ollie's not a young man."

A small laugh erupted from her throat. "That man can run me into the ground most days. But lately—do you think I'm looking for problems where there are none?"

"You've got a lot of things on your plate. Margaret, Ollie, me."

"Yeah, it seems that if I don't hold on to it, then it's going to change." Fear and uncertainty clawed at her. She hadn't said anything to anyone about her confrontation with Austin.

"You can't do that. Ask someone who's tried."

He'd hit the problem square on. "I hate it when people throw my words back in my face."

He grinned. "Stop worrying. It's my time to ride."

His upbeat words touched her, bringing a ray of hope to her heart.

"Let me close out this file and I'll be there."

Sophie quickly got out of her program and followed Zach out of the office. Who would've thought Zach would repeat her words back to her? Was she only seeing the problems and not the solution? She needed to trust God.

Lord, I'm confused and adrift here. Please be with me and give me wisdom, she prayed as she walked out of the office.

Sophie smiled at Zach as he sat in the saddle atop Prince Charming. He'd ridden Prince Charming around the ring several times. She saw glimpses of the old Zach in his eyes. His improvement had astounded her with its speed. But there was still more for him to do.

"You're looking good," Ethan called.

"Like an older brother who is a pain." Beth's smile radiated her pride.

Sophie stepped up to the ring's wooden rail. "You up for a new challenge?"

Zach stopped Prince Charming and rested his forearm on the saddle horn. "What do you have in mind?"

"How about saber practice? I hear you old-time cavalry guys love to practice charges."

Zach's spine straightened and his chest came up. "Yes, those of us who were in the mounted corp did that." His eyes narrowed, waiting.

She nodded. "You want to try doing that?"

He glanced around, looking for any target. "Sure, why not?"

"Okay, let me set it up." Moving toward Beth and Ethan, Sophie started issuing orders. "Ethan, I'll need you to put up all the horses in the back corral in their stalls. Ollie will help. Beth, in the tack room there's a hula hoop in the back corner behind the saddle blankets. Get that and bring it to that back corral."

Everyone started moving. It took ten minutes for them to rig up the arm and suspend the hula hoop on a rope from the arm of the inverted L-shaped pole at the entrance to the paddock beside the stables.

Zach rode out to the corral.

Sophie ran into the office and grabbed a plastic light saber in the corner that she'd picked up at the local warehouse club store. She handed it to Zach. It was orange and black.

"What do you want me to use this for?"

She heard Ethan sort behind her.

"Work with me here, Zach. I didn't have a real live saber, so I thought you could use this."

He frowned as he evaluated the toy. "You want me to use this?"

She thought this would be a great idea but he sounded like she wanted him to do backflips off the horse. "It's the best I could come up with at a moment's notice. I have the broken handle off a pitchfork if you want to use that, but I warn you the end is jagged."

Beth and Ethan stood to the side, waiting for Zach's answer. Ethan's mouth kept moving as he tried to bite back his grin. Ollie stood beside Sophie.

Zach studied his siblings, then stared down at the toy. He remained silent, fighting some sort of inner battle. Finally he said, "This will do."

The breath she'd been holding swished out.

"He's a smart man," Ollie said, his voice pitched low so only Sophie could hear.

She'd questioned herself on whether this would work, but Zach needed to be challenged. "When you want to bring a real saber, you're welcome, but I'd thought we'd start with this. Besides, the weight is better for your first try." She'd talked to the therapist, Captain Perry, at Brook Army Medical yesterday and asked for ideas to help Zach. The therapist told her about this setup for his patients to help with balance. The patient would have to balance himself on his legs and this would tell her if he had the strength.

Ethan grinned. "It looks good."

Zach ignored him and Beth elbowed Ethan.

"What?" Ethan complained.

Sophie disregarded Ethan's antics and focused on Zach. "They use this exercise at Brook Army as part of their soldiers' therapy."

"They use that?" Ethan asked.

Sophie turned and glared at Ethan. His grin disappeared.

"I don't know what sort of sword the army uses, but for now that will work," she said.

Zach studied the child's toy. "Starting small is probably a good idea."

Relief rushed through Sophie. Out of the corner of her eye, she saw Beth and Ethan smiling.

"The therapist was very high on this exercise. It helps with balance, control and having all your muscles work together."

"That's genius." Ethan turned to his brother. "Let's see if you can do it."

Zach couldn't resist the challenge from his brother. "Are you daring me, big brother?"

Ethan laughed. "You got it."

Zach turned Prince Charming around and rode him around the enclosure. Once, twice.

Sophie pushed fear out of her mind, just as she had when going out to get a wounded soldier in Iraq. Instead she focused on the goal and prayed that Zach was up to this challenge. The fear that maybe she should've waited for another week to allow Zach to build up his muscles tried to creep into her head, but she ruthlessly pushed it aside. He was a soldier. He'd faced the enemy before.

"But never himself." The whispered words floated in her brain.

On the third time around the ring, he lifted the plastic saber and thrust it at the hula hoop.

He missed and his body tipped toward his right side.

She held her breath. *Oh, Lord, help.*

Zach fought for his balance. He pulled his right arm in and managed to settle himself in the center of the saddle.

He turned around and grinned at Sophie.

Suddenly she realized Zach had used his core muscles, abdominal muscles and thighs to right himself in the saddle.

Her eyes filled with moisture but she wouldn't cry. She looked over at Beth and Ethan. From the looks on their faces, they also realized how much Zach had recovered.

Zach guided Prince Charming around for a second pass at the target. Zach raised the saber and rode toward the hula hoop. As he passed it, he thrust with his right hand. He didn't get the sword through the hoop, but he kept his balance.

Zach rode around the ring again and tried for the third time. He made it.

Cheers went up from his siblings.

"That's the prettiest thing I've seen in a long time," the whispered words came from behind her.

Sophie glanced over her shoulder to meet Ollie's gaze. "I couldn't agree more," she replied.

"You've done good, girl. That boy's on the mend."

She wanted to ask him how he felt, but Ollie moved away.

Zach made several more passes at the target and got the saber in two of the three times. As he guided Prince Charming to the gate, Sophie could see the pride and joy in his face.

"I like your friend's suggestion," Zach said.

"When he told me about that last night, I had my doubts, but he knew what he was talking about."

Zach patted Prince Charming on the neck. "And you did a great job, boy."

Prince Charming nodded his head.

Sophie heard a car in the parking lot. After the car stopped, and the doors opened, a little boy called out, "Hey, Miss Sophie. I'm here."

Sophie waved back. "I'm coming." Turning, she looked up at Zach. "You did great." She headed toward the stable office. She didn't need to worry about putting Prince Charming back in his stall. Zach would take care of things. That was one less thing she had to do.

Zach did more than just fill a need at the ranch. He gave her a glimpse of what might be to have him here at the ranch—working by her side as a permanent member of the staff.

Beth and Ethan followed Zach as he walked Prince Charming back to his stall.

Ethan clamped Zach on the back. He didn't say anything, but Zach knew his brother was proud. Things were beginning to come back into focus.

"I'd like to help with the chores, but Dad called before I got here. I've got to run some errands for him at the bank, and he wants it done this afternoon and doesn't want to wait until Monday."

"I understand."

"Dad also asked when he and Mom could come down and watch you ride."

Zach felt none of the panic that request would've brought a month ago, and he realized how far he'd come. *Thank You, Lord, for bringing Sophie into my life.*

Beth stood beside Ethan, her posture tight as if ready to leap in and smooth the situation.

"That's not a problem. Any day they want to drive down will be fine."

Beth relaxed. "They'll be excited."

With a final slap on Zach's back, Ethan walked away. When Beth started to follow, Zach put his hand on her arm, stopping her. "You have a few minutes?"

He waited.

"I have a meeting at three, but I've got time to talk," she said.

Zach tied Prince Charming to the ring by his stable and unsaddled him. He put it on the saddle rest in Prince Charming's stall.

Beth joined him with grooming the horse.

"This reminds me of when you and I had to work together for my 4-H project."

He remembered the time when he was helping her

with that particular venture. Beth had been in the eighth grade and he was in high school.

"What do you know about Sophie's family?" Zach asked as he ran the curry brush over Prince Charming's neck.

She paused and looked over the horse's back. "What brought that on?"

"I'm curious about her family. I know that Mom and Dad have called daily, wanting to come and watch me, wanting progress reports. And I'll admit, it's driven me crazy, but I know they care. But since I've been working here, I've wondered about Sophie's family." Sophie had mentioned nothing of her family and he knew of no contact between them. He wondered at the silence.

"I can't tell you much. Sophie didn't talk about them much. They called a couple of times a year, but it was mostly her grandmother that she talked to. I got the feeling her mother and grandmother weren't on good terms.

"She sometimes talked about her brother, Matt." Beth continued to brush Prince Charming, but her strokes were automatic and her eyes took on a faraway look. "Oh, there was one time, her grandmother came to visit. Sophie was glad to see her and they spent the day together. But other than that, I can't recall her family ever visiting."

"And since Sophie didn't go to the graduation ceremony, you didn't see them at that time," he added.

"It surprised me when Sophie told me she'd signed up for the army and was leaving after her last final exam for boot camp." She shrugged. "When I asked her about graduation, she said it didn't matter."

That troubled Zach. His family had been a bulwark for him. He knew he could count on them no matter what happened. They were there cheering for him when he walked across the auditorium stage at Eastern New Mexico State. And they cheered when he got his commission in the army.

Even though his parents had a tough time dealing with his injuries, Zach never doubted for an instant that his parents loved him and supported him.

"Do you have any idea what the trouble between them was?"

"Yeah." She set the curry brush on the table beside the stall. Running her hands along the side of Prince Charming, Beth seemed to debate with herself. Finally, she said, "It all revolved around her brother's death. She never told me what it was, but I know that there was the problem."

"Are you sure?"

"I'm sure."

"You're sure of what?" Sophie asked, walking toward them.

Beth's face lost all color. Her hand stilled on Prince Charming's side.

"She's sure she can't stay the afternoon and help with the chores," Zach smoothly supplied.

Beth's head came up. "That's right. I have a meeting—" she glanced at her watch "—in less than forty minutes at headquarters. I think I'll have just enough time to drive downtown." She kissed Zach's cheek.

"Good ride. And I think with a little practice, you'll get the hang of the saber thing."

She moved to Sophie and hugged her. "Thank you," she whispered. When Beth pulled back, her smile quivered. "Bye." Beth sprinted down the center of the stable and slipped out the open door beside the tack room.

"I was hoping you'd help with this new rider. One of my sidewalkers had a flat tire and won't be here for another hour. Could you help?"

"Sure. I'll put Prince Charming up and meet you at the mounting steps."

Over the next forty minutes, Zach walked beside the new rider. The little girl spent the first ten minutes crying, then suddenly like flipping a switch she decided she loved to ride and she wanted to be the horse's best friend.

When the sidewalker showed up, Zach let her take his place. His energy was spent.

Walking into the tack room, he sat on the stool by the front cabinet. A thousand different thoughts shot through his brain. Pride and excitement for his accomplishment flooded him. He had to laugh. Riding with a child's light saber was one of the best moments he'd had in a long time. He remembered doing that very exercise during his time in the mounted cavalry.

His smile slowly faded as he thought about Sophie. Ollie hadn't told her about his cancer. The man needed to level with her ASAP. Zach wanted to warn Sophie, but he'd made Ollie a promise. If Sophie looked close enough, she'd see something wasn't right with her old friend.

But the thing nagging at him the most was Sophie's mysterious relationship with her family. Something wasn't right. In all the time he'd been here, Sophie hadn't mentioned her parents. Not once. And he didn't think she'd gotten any calls or letters from them.

Why?

He felt a protectiveness rise up in him.

His stomach rumbled, reminding him he hadn't eaten before he rode. Zach walked to the office and got himself a bottle of water and one of the cookies Sophie kept in the cabinet above the mini-fridge.

By the time he finished off the third cookie, Ollie walked in.

"How are you feeling?" Zach asked the older man.

"Like I've been stomped by a bull." He raised his straw hat and ran his fingers through his steel-gray hair.

"Anything I can do for you?"

Ollie nodded toward the water. "Got another one of those?"

Zach grabbed another cold bottle of water and handed it to him. "Anything else I can do?"

"Nope, you're doing it by keeping things going here. Sophie's got enough to handle without me pouring more worry on it. I know that Margaret is out of the hospital, but she ain't come home. I'm expecting trouble from her kids."

"What kind of trouble?"

Ollie shrugged. "I think they might want us to stop giving lessons."

Zach looked out the window and saw Sophie as she

walked Brownie around the ring with a young girl on the horse's back. The girl had a leg brace on her leg. Hinged at the knee, the brace had red-and-white stripes on it with blue stars.

"I think it might be time for Sophie and me to go out and have dinner."

"I like your thinkin', young man. And you can discuss more than ranching." The old man's eyebrows wiggled.

Was Zach that transparent?

"Take the worry off your face, boy. I was just teasin' ya."

Ollie may have said he was teasing, but Zach got the distinct feeling Ollie was all for some "sparking" between Sophie and him. "I'll be sure not to call dinner a date. I'll tell her that we can talk shop."

Ollie grinned. "Good idea."

"I still think you should tell Sophie what's going on with you."

All humor left Ollie's face. "Not now."

"She's stronger than you think. If she was an army medic, she can handle a lot. I shudder to think of the things she saw. I know in quiet moments, I see too much."

Ollie remained quiet for several moments. "I know she can, but why put that burden on her? I'll fight this myself and won't borrow her strength."

"Ollie, haven't you read in Ecclesiastes that a three-fold cord isn't quickly broken? With Sophie and my strength, we can help you."

Ollie put his water down and joined Zach at the

window. "That may be, but I just can't tell her right now. Let's see how I'm doing after my next chemo."

Zach's first impulse was to argue with Ollie, but he would honor the older man's wishes. "It's your call."

Ollie nodded and walked out of the office. Zach followed. He had work to be done.

Chapter Seven

Sophie pulled the office door closed and put her key in the lock.

Friday night and what did she have planned? Going to the house and nuking another frozen dinner. Pretty pathetic. Wanting to avoid the empty house and kitchen, she decided to check the stock before she called it a night.

Walking into the stables, she heard Zach's voice.

"You did a nice job out there, boy. You would've made a great cavalry horse. I think the Union soldiers would've loved to have ridden you into any battle against the Indians out here."

"He's probably not going to answer you."

Zach turned and shrugged a sheepish smile on his lips.

"When I was in Iraq, our shrink kept a puppy that had wandered into camp one day. That little ball of fur got so many GIs to come in and just talk, vent their feelings or just relax. Amazing what an animal can do."

She leaned her forearms against the half wall of the stall

and studied Prince Charming. "I talk to my horses all the time. They know all my secrets." She turned her head. "You think Prince Charming knows what you're saying?"

"I don't know, but I've gotten a lot of head-bobbing and agreeing."

Sophie laughed. "And I'm sure he didn't talk back."

"You'd be surprised how much Prince Charming lets me know when he's not happy."

"That I don't doubt."

Zach patted Prince Charming on the neck. "Instead of me talking to this handsome devil, why don't I talk to you about how things are running?"

What was he asking? "Sure."

"I thought we might do it over dinner."

"If you're up to a frozen dinner, sure."

His laughter rolled through the stables. "If I want to talk, then I should spring for the food. How about we eat Mexican? You know any good places out here?"

"Yup."

"Okay, why don't I drive us there and we have dinner?"

Sophie's heart beat faster. "Okay. But let me follow you in my car, that way you won't have to come back here."

"No can do. I want to show you how much my leg has improved by showing off my driving skill. If you're in another car, you can't see that."

His request surprised her. "Okay. Let me finish looking at all the horses, then we can go."

Zach's satisfied smile made her wonder if this dinner was more than a business meeting. She could only hope.

Mama Juanita's Kitchen was a small house turned into a restaurant on the southeastern outskirts of Albuquerque. The large corner lot covered in gravel and dirt was filled with cars. An overflow of vehicles parked on the street and in the alley. Zach found a spot behind the house next to the big industrial trash bin.

The wonderful smell of chilies, beans and mouthwatering spices wafted out the front door. Sophie's stomach rumbled and her mouth watered. "I didn't realize how hungry I was."

"You've put in a long day." His stomach rumbled, too. "So have I. Those cookies I snatched out of the office weren't enough."

"Especially for a growing boy like you."

Zach grinned and wagged his brows.

They stopped by the greeter and before the woman could open her mouth, a voice from the back of the room called out. "Ah, *chica,* it is good to see you."

Sophie turned to the voice. Juanita Espinosa hurried to the front of the room and wrapped her arms around Sophie. Sophie towered over the short, round woman. With her salt-and-pepper hair pulled back into a bun and her ready smile, too many people thought Juanita was an easygoing happy woman who could be walked over. It didn't take them long to realize their mistake.

When Juanita let her go, she looked up at Zach.

"Who is this? Have you finally got a man in your life?" Juanita grinned.

Blood rushed to Sophie's cheeks. "Zach is helping out at the ranch while Margaret is gone."

"How is Margaret? I called the hospital, but they tell me she isn't there."

Juanita and Margaret had known each other for twenty years. Often, Margaret and Sophie would treat themselves and have dinner here. The three women would laugh and trade stories. Juanita and Margaret would often swap stories of their errant children and would ask to hear about Sophie's experiences in the army. In an odd sort of way, Sophie had become their adoptive child.

Sophie slipped her hands into the back pockets of her jeans. "Austin put her in an extended-stay home for therapy."

"That boy," Juanita exclaimed. "He needs someone to grab him by the ear and sit him down and give him a good talking-to. That daughter who is still here—" She shook her head. "The only good child she had moved to Oregon.

"Come. I've got a special seat for you at the back. I'll come and join you when I can."

They wound their way through the tables to the back corner. A lit candle provided most of the light for the table.

"Sit and I'll tell your waiter to bring you the special." She disappeared into the kitchen.

"I don't get a menu?" Zach asked.

"You can have one if you want one, but I'll guarantee you that you're going to want her special."

He leaned back and studied her. After a moment, he nodded. "I'll trust you."

Oddly enough, she knew he'd been trusting her for the past couple of weeks. His recovery had been near miraculous. "You won't be disappointed."

"I haven't been so far."

Her brows wrinkled. "Meaning?"

"You've been right about therapy and riding. If you say 'the special' is something I'll like, I'll believe you."

Suddenly dinner seemed like a date. And her stomach decided to keep tempo with the upbeat music playing in the background. Her brain went blank and her tongue seemed to swell.

A waiter showed up with two glasses of iced tea and a bowl of fried corn tortilla chips and salsa. She snatched up a chip, dipped it into the salsa and popped it into her mouth.

The chip went down the wrong way and she started to choke. Instantly, Zach's hand slapped her on the back. The chip dislodged and went down. She grabbed her tea and took a drink.

"Thanks," she croaked.

"No problem. Is the salsa that good?"

Smiling through her embarrassment, she nodded. "It is. It's just the chip went down the wrong way."

He picked up a chip and ran it through the salsa. He popped it into his mouth. "Excellent."

Sophie felt like an idiot. She couldn't eat a chip without choking.

"I want to thank you for the light saber today."

She latched onto the change in topic. "I couldn't think of anything else to use. It was better than the broken handle of the pitchfork."

"After I got over the shock, I liked the challenge. And I'm sure I'll hear from my parents about today's exercise."

"I hope you're not complaining about your caring family."

He paused with a chip in his hand. "No, I'm not."

"Good. Be grateful. They might've approached things wrong after you came home from the hospital," his face took on a mulish quality, "but as I recall your parents have good hearts."

When he opened his mouth, she leaned forward and whispered, "Remember, I was your sister's roommate. She told me a lot of things that her brothers did."

He leaned back in his chair and his eyes narrowed. "What exactly did she tell you?"

She had him worried. Good. Of course some of the stories Beth shared, she had her part in the adventure. There was one time when the boys snuck out to go to a cave in the mountain above their ranch. Beth had followed and ended up falling and breaking her arm, and her brothers had carried her home.

"I think I'll keep those secrets. Remember, your parents had a couple of wild boys, but they loved them through it."

Before he could respond, the waiter appeared with

two plates. On the plate was a chili relleno covered with a light green sauce. Refried beans and rice filled up the rest of the plate.

Sophie leaned over her plate and whispered, "Try it. The sauce is excellent."

He eyed her.

"Trust me."

Cutting the relleno, he forked a bite into his mouth. He smiled. "You're right again."

Her eyes locked with his and Sophie knew she'd lost her heart.

Zach wolfed down the relleno. Her little mention about knowing about his misadventures rattled him. And of course, those adventures fell into two categories— pre-teen and teen. What had Beth told her? There were lots of things that he didn't want his folks to know about what Ethan and he'd done. What he needed to do was find a way to talk about her family.

Leaning forward, he said, "Since you know about my secrets, don't you think I'm entitled to know some of yours?"

Sophie put her fork down and picked up her iced tea. After a drink, she sat back. "Why would I want to tell you about my misadventures?"

"To humor me?"

Her gaze searched his. "Once when I was six and my brother was nine, he took my Barbie and hid it because I was using his favorite truck for Barbie's car. He took his car back and I got so mad. I threw his shoes at him. My aim wasn't good and I missed him and his shoe hit a vase in the living room and broke it. Mom thought Matt threw the shoe. He didn't rat me out and took the blame." She fell silent.

His hand covered hers and lightly squeezed.

Her gaze met his. "I still miss him. It was as if the light went out in our family when he died."

Zach heard the rumors on the rodeo circuit that Matt had been killed in some sort of riding accident, but he didn't know the details. Sophie had told Beth her brother died when she was twelve, but no one knew exactly what happened.

She shook her head as if shaking off the sad memories. "Thank you for filling the hole when my sidewalker was late."

With her change in subject, Zach knew the door had been closed and he wouldn't push her further. He sensed a wound or tenderness that Sophie let few people see. He knew that she wouldn't have shown that weakness in the army.

"I'm glad I had the energy to do it."

Juanita came to the table holding two plates. Sopapillas. "I wanted to bring you the finishing touch of your dinner." She placed the puffy cinnamon-and-sugar-coated fried pastries on the table.

It had been close to ten years since he had a sopapilla. "This is a treat, Juanita. And the rest of the meal was excellent."

The older woman nodded her thanks. "You need to keep this one, Sophie. Manners are few and far between these days."

Sophie's smiled weakly. "He's a good worker."

Juanita settled in the empty chair at the table and chatted with Sophie for a few minutes. The tension in her shoulders eased. He didn't know that tension resulted in Juanita's matchmaking or his questions about her family. But his plan to learn more about this woman had run into a serious roadblock.

What was Sophie hiding? Because in his experience, people who shared nothing of themselves often hid wounds they didn't want anyone to see.

Zach parked his truck by the guesthouse. Sophie smiled as she watched him drive with his right leg.

"I'm impressed," she said after he shut off the engine.

"I've been practicing. When I go home after I finish here, I take my truck out to a dirt road by my condo and practice driving. It's a good thing that when I bought this baby I decided to get an automatic. When I was at Walter Reed, Dad wanted to have the truck fitted with hand controls, but I refused." He shrugged. "Maybe it was vanity, but I was going to drive this the regular way."

He certainly worked to strengthen his muscles. "It was a goal, and you worked to achieve it," Beth said. He worked like a man possessed.

She got out of the truck, ready to say good-night, but he followed her up the walk and stepped onto the front porch. A cane-back rocker sat on the porch surrounded by two whiskey barrels filled with pansies and snapdragons. The crispness of the air made her aware of all her senses. The comforting smells of horse and hay danced in the wind. Suddenly, Zach stepped close, filling all her senses. His tall form hovered over her, and she could feel the heat of him. Dinner took on a new dimension. This felt like a date, and dates usually ended with a kiss.

Feeling self-consciousness and shy, she said, "I called the army representatives yesterday to see when they could come out and observe your training. The colonel in charge told me he'd give me a call in the next day or so."

His eyes grew dark with emotion. "Don't worry about it."

"I wish I could, but this is too important." Hugging her waist, her hands moved up and down her upper arms. "I've been praying the Lord would help us establish this therapy program, but there'd been so many roadblocks thrown in the way. First Margaret's stroke, then Ollie disappears and when he comes back, he seems off."

"But He sent me."

Sophie felt her mouth go slack.

"Uh, that came out wrong."

"You think?"

"What I meant was I was the perfect test case for the army. I've got connections I might be able to use to help you."

He had a point. The Lord couldn't have sent a better example. "Well, if you could talk to someone that would be great because the colonel I contacted didn't seem eager to come out here, and I don't understand that. Before, he seemed so interested to see what riding could do for the men."

Zach grinned back at her. He stepped closer and lightly brushed back a lock of hair that came loose from her braid. "Maybe his superior chewed him out that day. I know that's happened to me when I got chewed on. What you have to do is keep your head down and keep going."

Sophie saw his mouth moving, but she was concentrating on his fingers putting those stray tendrils behind her ears. "Uh-huh."

His gaze captured hers. "Give me his name, and I'll call." With each word, his mouth moved closer and closer until his lips brushed across hers.

Once.

Twice.

When she didn't object, his mouth settled firmly on hers and his arms slipped around her back, drawing her close to him. Her eyes fluttered closed. All the times she'd imagined Zach kissing her didn't hold a candle to the real thing. He curled her toes.

When he pulled back, his eyes were soft and his smile broad.

She needed to respond to him, but words failed her. The phone inside the house rang, saving her from having to say anything. She unlocked the door and rushed inside. Zach followed.

Snatching the phone off the kitchen wall, she blurted, "Hello."

"Sophie. This is Lynda McClure."

Zach's mother. Sophie's gaze flew to Zach's. "Hello, Mrs. McClure."

Zach's eyes widened.

"I was hoping we might have dinner with you tomorrow night. We heard from Beth about Zach's progress today and wanted to know more."

Sophie watched as Zach reacted as she talked. "You could talk with Zach and ask him questions."

"I intend to, but I think we'd get a better picture if we talked to you, a more unbiased observer," Lynda replied.

Zach held out his hand. Sophie shook her head.

"Hey, Mom," he called out.

"Is that Zach? He's there?"

Sophie surrendered the phone.

"Hello, Mom." As he listened, his brow rose. "I think that's a good idea. I'll ask her." He covered the mouth piece. "You want to have dinner with my folks?"

The situation could be a powder keg. "I won't talk to them without your approval. It's up to you. If you want me to talk to them, I'll do it."

He put the phone back to his ear. "Okay, Mom." His mother said something that made him frown. "Driving all that way is a lot to ask. Why don't we meet at someplace north of the city?"

Nodding, he listened. "That sounds great, Mom. We'll see you at seven." He hung up and turned to her. "I talked her out of dinner at the ranch. We'll meet them at my mother's favorite restaurant in Albuquerque." He stepped to her side. "You sure you don't mind?"

"No. I've always liked your parents."

"Good night, Sophie. Be prepared for an inquisition tomorrow night, but at least you can comfort yourself with the best steaks in Albuquerque."

She hoped it would be that easy.

It probably wouldn't be. She wasn't known for her dazzling conversational skills or her wonderful speeches. But she could talk horses, how therapy worked, its benefits and Zach's progress. But she wouldn't mention what a marvelous kisser he was. That would certainly bring all the dinner conversation to a screeching halt.

Chapter Eight

As Sophie watched Zach drive out of the parking lot, she suddenly felt overwhelmed. She stumbled through the front door, locking it. Her head rested against the door, she wondered what was happening. Dinner with Zach's parents tomorrow night was simply business. They wanted to know about their son's progress. Nothing more.

Walking to the kitchen table, she collapsed into one of the chairs. So, why did she feel so confused? Zach's kiss.

Obviously, Zach had feelings for her as proven by what just happened, but where had those feelings sprung from? Gratitude. Simple gratitude to his therapist for his recovery. Nothing more.

She'd pushed him into riding again, forced him to face the life he'd left. She expected him to ride, to be the man he was before the blast. She didn't operate from pity. She demanded the best from him and didn't accept excuses.

He responded to that tough love with an eagerness that surprised her.

So had he misinterpreted his own feelings?

And what about her feelings? Zach tapped into the attraction she felt for him so long ago, but watching him struggle, and watching him interact with the kids and Ollie, she gained a respect for the man. She admired him. That was it. Nothing more.

Too bad that logic didn't feel right.

Unlocking the front door, she raced to the stable and walked to Prince Charming's stall.

"Well, boy. I've got a problem." He came to the half door and nudged her hand, wanting her to stroke his nose.

"What am I going to do?" She rested her head on his neck. "I don't know what Zach's feelings are, but I'm sure he can't identify his feelings any more than I can."

Sophie'd been burned before and now she needed to guard her heart. She'd been halfway through her first tour in Iraq when the army sent her back to D.C. to learn the latest updated field techniques for battlefield injuries. She met an army captain, Bryan Denison, who'd lost both of his legs, but was recuperating and doing equine therapy. Sophie fell in love with Bryan and thought he loved her, too. They'd spent the two weeks that she'd been in D.C. together. When she wasn't in class, she was at the stable or in the hospital with Bryan.

The day before she was to ship back to Iraq, she went to Bryan's room in the hospital to spend her last night before she deployed. When she walked into the room,

Bryan had his arms around a woman, and he was kissing her. When they came up for air, he introduced his fiancée to her.

If she'd been hit by an eighteen-wheeler, Sophie couldn't have been more flattened. When she quickly excused herself and fled into the hall, Bryan followed her and told her he was sorry she'd misread his feelings. He gently explained he did have feelings for her, but they were feelings of gratitude and thankfulness.

One of the shrinks had seen the scene in the hallway. He'd taken her arm and escorted her to his office. There he told her that she had to be careful to separate professional and personal feelings and that if she didn't, this wouldn't be the only time her feelings would be misread by the patient or herself. Even friendship with a patient carried danger. It was a good thing to have friendship with a recovering patient, but any relationship that developed in this stressed situation could be misconstrued by either party. She needed to guard her heart and to be sure her patients didn't mistake their gratitude for love.

She'd learned a valuable lesson that day. Never mix the two.

This worried her about Zach. Was he mistaking gratitude for something else? She knew her feelings were the real thing, but she couldn't be sure his were.

When Zach arrived home, his answering-machine light blinked. Before he could check the messages, his phone rang. He answered.

"Son, you need to buy a cell phone," his mother exclaimed.

He readied himself for the third degree. "Okay."

"I hope you're not upset about me inviting Sophie to dinner. Beth couldn't stop talking about how much progress you're making. Why, even Ethan bragged about you and I thought you probably wouldn't want to talk about it, so I thought I could get answers from Sophie."

Oddly, Zach wasn't upset with his mother's tactics. "What Beth and Ethan said must've been spectacular to have you call Sophie."

"When Ethan told your father and me about that thing with the hula hoop, I laughed. Your dad even commented that it was a smart idea."

Zach stretched out in his big leather chair. He remembered seeing that red hoop waving in the breeze and it made him smile. At first he thought Sophie had lost her mind. What was he going to do with a light saber, he wondered, but once he got over the foolish feelings, he wanted to do the exercise they did in the mounted cavalry.

Her idea had been a stroke of genius.

"I'll say she surprised me."

"Well, you can fill in all the details at dinner tomorrow night."

"Be nice when you pump Sophie for all the details of my progress," he teased.

His mother remained quiet. "Do you think I'd do that to her?"

His conscience pricked him. "Yes, but that's why I love you."

"Thank you."

"Then we'll see you around five?"

"See you tomorrow, son. And I am so grateful to the Lord for the good things that are happening. Do you know He's got a plan for you? It might not be the one you thought it was, but He doesn't desert His children."

"I know, Mom." He hung up.

He knew God had a plan for him, but he still didn't know what that plan was. He knew it had changed. And suddenly, he thought about a future with a wife.

He dialed his sister and got Sophie's number at the guesthouse. The phone rang several times and Zach began to worry about Sophie's safety. On the sixth ring she picked up.

"I was getting ready to drive back out to the ranch and check on you."

"Sorry, I was out checking the horses."

"Talking to Prince Charming?"

Her laughter made him smile. "Guilty as charged."

"That horse is the best listener in the business. You should just hang out a shingle, Horse Psychologist."

"That's an idea."

"The reason I called is I want to make sure you're okay with talking to my parents tomorrow night. I know Beth has been bragging about your genius. I think Ethan echoed Beth's excitement."

"I'm fine. Remember, I know your folks and how they feel about their children."

"You're not doing this because you feel backed into a corner, are you, because if you are, then we'll cancel the dinner."

"Zach, I'm okay with it."

"They'll have a thousand questions, want your evaluation of my progress, want an overview of what's happening. I guess they wouldn't believe me."

"I'm okay with it, Zach." She chuckled. "As I recall, your folks won't put any thumbscrews on me."

"Don't say I didn't warn you."

"I'll consider myself warned."

He wanted to continue talking to her. He felt like a teen with his first crush. "I thought we might try having dinner again. And not with my parents."

She remained quiet.

"On the drive to the restaurant we could plan a strategy on how to get the army contract."

"That's a plan."

He breathed a sigh of relief. "I'll see you tomorrow. And, Sophie, I had a good time tonight."

"I did, too."

After the goodbyes, she hung up.

Zach stared at the phone. Oddly enough, he knew his mother had done him a favor by asking for Sophie to come to dinner. The arguments he gave Sophie were the bald truth. He didn't want to field any of those questions his parents would have, and Sophie would handle them better than he could.

He found himself looking forward to driving out to the restaurant tomorrow night. His mind wandered back to the kiss he shared with Sophie.

The heart he thought had shriveled up and died suddenly made itself known. His high school girlfriend, he later learned, had only wanted his father's connections to the movers and shakers in Taos, only wanted to advance her career in public relations. And his college girlfriend had abandoned him the moment he was commissioned in the army. He didn't fit into her plans for advancement.

Walking into the bedroom, he sat on the bed and removed his prosthesis, setting it by the nightstand. His leg had healed nicely. Looking down at what was left of his leg came the nagging fear of what Sophie would think after seeing it. He wouldn't allow his parents to see the stump. Ethan had seen it, but that was because he helped Zach in the beginning with putting on the prosthesis.

The army shrinks told him how to deal with others' emotions and reactions, but it was his roommate in the hospital that had helped him the most. Talk to God is what Bill told him to do.

The urge to talk to his friend hit him. He picked up the phone and called Bill.

"Hey, friend, how are you doing?" Bill asked.

Zach told him about his weeks at the ranch.

"I wish I could've done that. I think it would've made my recovery easier."

"Check around you, Bill. You might have something there in Lubbock."

"I will. Is that the reason you called, friend? Wanted me to start equine therapy?"

Bill saw right through him. "No. I have a couple of questions. What was your wife's reaction to seeing you without your prosthesis?"

Bill laughed. "The only reason I can think you'd

be asking me *that* particular question is you've found someone."

"I don't kiss and tell."

"Oh-ho. I'm right. Well, Terri's reaction was to thank God that I'm alive. She's grateful I lived. She's never been repulsed by the sight of my stumps."

The weight on Zach's shoulders lifted.

"My mother cried, but I knew she was glad I was alive. After my daughter's first look at it, she asked, 'Does it hurt?' When I told her sometimes, she nodded, accepted and went on. It didn't faze her."

"I can believe that. I've been working with a little boy who thinks my leg makes me special."

"Kids are great."

Too bad all folks didn't react the way Andy did.

"Since you're working with equine therapy, have you talked to anyone at Walter Reed? Folks might want to know about where you're working."

"No, but that's a good idea. Thanks."

"Zach, don't let that missing leg define your life. If it's the right lady, it won't bother her."

Bill's words rang through his head as he reached for his crutches. After he finished in the bathroom, he slid into bed.

Sophie knew who he was, and she'd been working with who he is now.

His feelings for Sophie made him want more. He'd see how she'd held up to his parents' inquisition tomorrow night. If she could handle them, then she probably could handle anything.

Hope filled his heart.

* * *

Sophie hurried and dressed. How she slept so late, she didn't know, but she needed to get to the stable.

"Okay, Lord, I know why," she said as she grabbed a muffin and banana from the kitchen counter. She hurried out the front door toward the ranch office. Ollie pulled up in his truck. He was running late, too.

"Morning," Sophie called out.

Ollie grunted a greeting.

He looked pale this morning. His gait wasn't as steady as it normally was.

She moved to his side. "Are you feeling all right this morning?"

"I'm okay."

She wanted to argue with him, but if he wanted to show up here, she wouldn't make a fuss. But something wasn't right with the man. He'd never been as sick as he had been these past few weeks. "I'm going to run interference for Zach tonight with his parents."

That got Ollie's attention. "What?"

"Zach's mom heard about our exercise yesterday and wants to know more about it. I'm to explain what is going on to them."

"Good for you. I think you've done something special for that boy."

Sophie wanted to laugh at Ollie's use of "that boy," but she guessed from Ollie's view, Zach was a boy. "It's as if God sent Zach here to heal and help us establish the program for vets."

"I think you're right."

They walked toward the office. "Would you like some coffee?"

"Sure, bring me a cup."

They split up and she went to the office and Ollie walked into the stable. She heard the horses greet him.

She quickly made coffee and checked the schedule for today. She ate her muffin and poured herself a cup of coffee, gulping it down before she poured herself a second cup and Ollie his first.

Taking the mugs outside, she found him working in the tack room. She left the mug there and walked down the hall to greet each of the horses. Sam and Prince Charming always loved a greeting and pat in the morning.

She put the halter on Sam and brought her to the mounting steps. Walking to the tack room, she heard someone retching.

Looking into the tack room, she didn't see Ollie.

Whoever was throwing up continued to be sick. Sophie walked out of the stable and saw Ollie bent over. He stood on the side of the stable.

Racing to his side, Sophie put her hand on Ollie's back.

He looked at her and she saw the bleakness in his eyes.

"Let me help you to the office."

He didn't object, and that frightened Sophie more than anything else.

Once he settled in a chair, Sophie caught another chair and pulled it up to Ollie.

"What's wrong? And don't tell me it's a stomach virus."

Ollie wouldn't look her in the eye.

She grabbed his hand and held it. "Ollie, you can tell me anything. You're as close as my dad to me."

His eyes met hers. "Don't say that, because you don't talk to your father."

She gasped; his words nearly knocked her out of her chair.

"I'm sorry, Sophie. That wasn't right of me."

She wouldn't duck the truth. "You're right. I need to call my parents, but that's not going to tell me what's wrong with you."

He scratched the back of his neck. "I'm sick. Got cancer."

Shock and grief ran through her. "When did you discover it?"

"Right after Margaret had her stroke, I had bad stomach pains for a couple of weeks. I went to the doctor, thinking I might need something for an ulcer. He ran some tests and told me it was cancer. They operated and took out a tumor. Now I've got those torture treatments. Makes me sick for days. I can't even enjoy coffee."

"Why didn't you tell me?"

"'Cause you got enough problems without worrying about me. I wasn't going to put you into that hole. You need to be thinkin' about those kids and not some old coot."

Tears gathered in her eyes. "That's where you're wrong. You're my friend. More like a family member who's there to help." Snatching the tissue from the box on the desk, she wiped her eyes. "You are part of this team, and we share. If nothing else, I can pray."

Ollie grasped Sophie's hand. "That's why I know God sent Zach here. He's helping keep things together. And you're helping him."

His words struck a chord in her heart. "You're right. I think the Lord knew what we needed." She bit her bottom lip, praying for the right words to say to her friend. "You work as much as you like, but if you feel after a treatment you can't, don't come in. Call. We have several more volunteers coming. They won't replace you, but Zach seems good at directing them."

Ollie started to stand, but his legs gave out on him.

"Would you like to use the sofa in the guesthouse to lie down and take a nap?"

He shook his head. "Naw. I just need a little time to get my stomach right."

Glancing at her watch, she knew she needed to get back outside and saddle Sam. "Take your time, Ollie."

Over the next hour and a half, Sophie didn't have time to dwell on the news Ollie just gave her. Between the volunteers that needed to be directed and the kids and parents, every moment was filled.

Zach worked along with her, but she caught him stealing glances at her.

Ollie appeared and moved slowly about. He didn't act as a sidewalker, but helped with the horses.

After she finished working with her third rider, Sophie slipped into the office, telling herself it was for a bottle of water. She opened the mini-fridge and stared at the bottles of water. Tears filled her eyes and she couldn't see anything in front of her.

Lord, Lord, why?

She didn't remember closing the fridge door, or when Zach came into the office, but somehow she felt her face pressed against Zach's chest.

"Shh, Sophie." He lightly ran his hand over her back.

"Ollie has cancer," she said between sobs.

"I know."

It took several moments for Zach's words to sink in. When they did, she pulled back and looked at him. "You know?"

His fingers wiped away the tears. "He told me."

She stepped away from him. "And you've been keeping that a secret?"

"Ollie asked me to. He's worried that with Margaret's illness, it would be too much for you to have to worry about."

Anger flared to life. "How dare you not tell me something that important."

"Ollie asked me not to tell you. I gave my word."

"I don't care. You should've told me," she spat back.

"My word is my bond. I told Ollie that you needed to know, but he didn't want to tell you."

She wanted to yell at him, to tell him he should've told her, no matter his promise. Her conscience pricked her, letting her know she was being unreasonable. She wasn't ready to be reasonable yet. The hurt was too fresh. Instead, she turned around and walked out of the office. The next rider was here.

* * *

Zach worked with Red, a six-year-old mare that the younger children rode. He sprayed her down after her session and led her back to her stall.

He worked, trying not to think of how mad Sophie had been. He knew she felt betrayed. He prayed she would realize no one had betrayed her, but Ollie simply wanted to spare her the additional worry about his cancer.

Since Red was finished for the day, she needed to be groomed and fed. After he brushed her and rubbed her down, he walked to the feed room. Sophie stopped him before the door.

"I'm sorry for yelling at you."

"I understand. I was a convenient target. You couldn't yell at Ollie."

She leaned against the wall. "Am I doing the right thing here, Zach? It seems that major obstacles are being thrown in my way. Should I just quit after we finish these sessions?"

He touched her chin. "You think Moses wanted to give up the first time he asked Pharaoh to let the children of Israel go? Or the second time? Or the third time? Things got worse before they got better.

"And what of all those soldiers you want to help heal from their injuries? And are you going to leave Andy high and dry?"

"You know how to play dirty, don't you?"

He grinned. "That's not playing dirty. It's telling you that you have a mission. Don't give up. I know you've worked hard to save soldiers in Iraq, and you told them to fight, not give up, because their survival depended on their will to live. That was the key—the will to live. You've got that will, Sophie. And—" his eyes danced with delight "—you've got that in spades."

He saw the resolve enter her beautiful blue eyes. "You're right. I shouldn't complain, because neither Margaret nor Ollie is giving up. I don't have the right to give up, either."

He gave her a thumbs-up.

"Thank you." She leaned up and gave him a quick kiss on the lips.

"Miss Sophie, I'm here." A little girl stood in the broad entranceway to the stable. Her eyes were big and she'd obviously seen the kiss Sophie gave him.

Sophie looked back at him.

Zach wanted to return Sophie's kiss, but with an audience, he knew he couldn't. "Your next rider's waiting for you."

Sophie gave his hand a final squeeze before walking toward the little girl.

Zach's heart nearly failed when Sophie asked if she should give up, if she was on the wrong road. He knew things weighed heavily on her but he didn't realize how much. He knew—and his heart and spirit confirmed it—that she was on the right road.

That "feeling" had happened several times in Iraq, when everything looked right, but something inside him shouted no. Other times, others said they were going the wrong way on a patrol, but he'd kept going and as it turned out, they'd avoided a problem.

The day he'd been caught by the roadside bomb, his

spirit had been unsettled. He radioed his base that they were going to retreat and go a different direction to patrol that part of the section of Mosel when the bomb went off. Obviously, the insurgents had been watching them. Listening to his gut had saved most of his men and saved the little boy who'd approached the patrol for the usual chocolate they gave the kids.

It'd been a hard lesson to learn, listening to his gut. But he learned it well. He didn't want Sophie to regret her decision not to go forward with her dream.

She was on the right road.

Chapter Nine

Sophie clutched her purse in her hands and glanced over at Zach who sat behind the steering wheel of his pickup. "What do you want me to tell your parents?"

"Tell them the truth." He lifted his right shoulder. "I've got nothing to hide."

"Then why did you need me?"

He stared out at the oncoming traffic. "Sometimes it's easier for a person who isn't a relative to tell parents news than it is for the son or daughter."

She couldn't argue that. She wished that some- one would've talked to her parents after her brother's death.

"I want you to understand that I'll answer honestly and won't sugarcoat anything," she pressed, wanting him to recognize she'd give an honest evaluation.

"I wouldn't expect anything else."

She nodded and looked out the window. Ollie's news still weighed heavily on her heart. She kept offering up prayers for his recovery.

The sign for the Golden Door came into view. They

quickly parked and went inside. Sophie had never been to the upscale steak place in the northwestern part of the city. Once inside, it took a moment for her eyes to adjust to the dim light. Soft music floated through the air and the tables were set with crystal water glasses and tablecloths. The detailed wood paneling reminded Sophie of an old English pub.

Zach's parents waved at them from a corner table. They moved across the wooden floor to the table. Both his mother and father rose and hugged Zach. Lynda McClure was a beautiful woman who stood only a few inches shorter than her husband's towering form. Lynda's blue eyes quickly scanned her son. Sophie caught Zach's father checking out how his son looked. From the slight nod of approval, Ken McClure approved of his son's progress.

"You look wonderful," Lynda exclaimed, kissing her son on the cheek.

"The work agrees with you." Zach's father patted him on the back.

Lynda moved to Sophie and enveloped her in a big hug. "It's good to see you," she whispered. When she pulled back, Sophie could see the gratitude shining in Lynda's eyes. His father grabbed Sophie's hand and gave it a squeeze. "Hello, young lady." He stepped back. "You've become a beautiful young woman."

Sophie blushed.

As they settled around the table, the waitress came and took their orders. When she left, Lynda said, "Tell us how Zach's doing."

Before Sophie could answer, Beth and Ethan walked

into the restaurant. The hostess moved the group to a bigger table and after their orders were taken, Sophie answered Lynda's question.

Throughout the meal, Ethan and Beth added their comments on how Zach had improved. Both his parents asked thoughtful, probing questions.

Zach's siblings praised him on his riding and work around the ranch.

"Mom, you should've seen him with that plastic light saber," Beth added after describing what happened on the last riding session. "I didn't know whether to laugh or cry when Sophie walked out of the office with it." Beth turned to Zach. "The look on your face was price-less." She patted Zach's hand. "Once you got over your initial shock, you gave it a try. I was awed. And proud. And you know what, this morning I tried something similar using a broom handle, and I'm telling you, it's not easy."

Zach's dad laughed. "That's what you were doing this morning on your horse? I choked on my coffee as I was looking out the kitchen window."

Beth's cheeks turned beet-red.

"I thought you'd lost your mind and I called your mother, asking her what that was about. Had you lost your job or had some sort of trauma I didn't know about? She said no. I wasn't going to ask you what you were doing because I was afraid I might have to contact a head doctor for you."

His comment brought chuckles from all at the table.

"I knew Zach's progress had gotten to a place where

he needed a challenge." Sophie took up the conversation, enjoying the back and forth of this wonderful family. "I have to admit it wasn't my idea. When I called down to Brook Army, the therapist there gave me the idea. The guy I talked to had several more ideas on how to help build up Zach's strength. But I also think Zach's working around the ranch helping with the chores has built up his strength." Sophie smiled at Zach, wanting him to know how much she appreciated his actions.

He smiled back.

All four of the others at the table traded looks. She wondered if she had anything on her face.

"The kids love him," Sophie added, wanting to break the tension. "One of my little boys told his friends about Zach's fake foot. He's had to show it to several of the other kids."

Lynda's mouth opened and Ken's eyebrow shot up.

"We're going to have a sort of graduation a week from Wednesday." Sophie looked around the table. "You should come and see the kids. It's amazing."

"Thank you for the invitation. I'd like to attend." Lynda turned to her husband. "Wouldn't you?"

"I would."

Beth and Ethan also wanted to be there.

Sophie excused herself and walked to the restroom. She felt as if she'd run a marathon and wanted a moment alone. Stopping in front of the sink, Sophie stared into the mirror. She didn't have anything on her face, which she'd feared she might have. Opening her mouth, she checked her teeth to make sure nothing was stuck there.

Looked good.

So the reason Zach's parents were staring at her was something she said? Something she said to Zach?

Lord, I see the love Zach's parents have. I wish—

The restroom door opened and Lynda walked into the room.

"Have we overwhelmed you?" Lynda asked, walking to Sophie's side.

Sophie turned and faced the older woman. "No. I'm thankful that Zach has your support, but—"

"But we were making it easy for him not to challenge himself? Enablers?"

Lynda understood what she'd been doing.

"Yes."

"That's why I wanted to thank you. You've shaken us out of our despair and made us do some soul-searching. I've prayed, asking God to help all of us, and He sent you. Thank you."

That news unsettled Sophie. "Beth was instrumental. If she hadn't brought Zach, then none of this would've happened."

Lynda nodded. "My little girl is a wonder."

A longing sprang up in Sophie's heart, seeing the affection Lynda had for her daughter. If only her mother felt that way about her....

The door opened again and Beth slipped into the room. She looked from her mother to Sophie. "Everything okay?"

Lynda laughed and pulled her daughter into her arms.

* * *

Zach watched his mother disappear into the women's restroom after Sophie. Alarm bells went off in his head. None of the people at the table said anything, but after a few minutes of uncomfortable silence, Beth excused herself and left.

Ethan glanced at his sister's back. "I wonder if mother's grilling Sophie some more over details of your therapy." He leaned over his plate. "You think Beth went to referee the conversation?"

Ken took the final piece of bread and slathered it with butter. "You know better than that, son. Your mama wouldn't do anything like that."

"True," Ethan acknowledged. "Mom won't nail Sophie with questions, but she'll find out what she wants to know, no matter what."

Truer words were never spoken, Zach thought. His mother wasn't confrontational, but Lynda McClure knew how to get information from an individual and she knew how to get her way. His father often lamented about being nailed by her talent more than once. Each of Lynda's children had been on the wrong end of their momma's questioning.

Ken settled his forearms on the table. "I'm glad Sophie's challenged you, son." He directed his words at Zach. "And I'm proud of you for taking up the challenge. I see the man I knew."

His father's words settled in his heart, bringing Zach's chin up in pride. "Thank you. That's what Sophie wants to do for other vets. Help soldiers find out who they are. She cut me no slack and expected me to be honest with her."

Ken's mouth pressed into a line.

Seeing his father's reaction, Zach realized how his words sounded. "I didn't mean—"

Ken waved off his son's apology. "We needed to be honest with you, son. The problem was we didn't know how to act."

Ethan laughed. "Be careful what you wish for, little brother, because you might get an earful."

Both his dad and brother had nailed him. God had been dealing with his heart. His family hadn't known how to cope with what had happened. He didn't know how to, either, so he got mad. At that point he didn't know what his future held, but he knew now he needed to work and get stronger.

"You're right. Sometimes what we think we want isn't really what we need. But you need to pray that we can get this program up and running for other wounded vets. I know it will make a difference."

Before Ken could respond, the ladies rejoined them at the table.

His mother had an angelic smile on her face. Sophie looked fine, no worse for wear, and Beth grinned. That made Zach nervous.

As they drove away from the restaurant, Zach stole a glance at Sophie, trying to gauge her reaction to the night. She seemed lost in thought.

"Your parents are great," she mumbled.

"You think so?"

Her head jerked around and Sophie realized she

must've spoken aloud. "Yeah. I've always been impressed with your mom and dad."

"Sometimes they're a little overprotective."

"Well, they could've gone in the opposite direction and not cared." The instant the words were out of her mouth, she clamped her lips together. Apparently, she said something she hadn't meant to say.

He ignored her embarrassment. "You've got a point, but sometimes they can be suffocating. I know Beth wasn't happy with them when her first date showed up at the house and my parents spent close to thirty minutes grilling him." He shook his head. "I thought the boy would swallow his tongue before they allowed them to leave for the date."

"Beth knows that's love."

"That's not the reaction she had at the time." He laughed. "I think Beth's reaction scared the poor boy more than my parents did."

"I can imagine. I only saw Beth mad once in the years we roomed together. It's not something I want to see again."

"See, I have a point."

"You do, but that's not the way a girl wants her date to go."

"Are you speaking from personal experience?"

The truck cab fell silent. She shook her head and looked out the door window.

They could go in the opposite direction and not care.

The words echoed in his brain.

Her tension reached out to him, making him wonder

if her parents were the ones who didn't care. From what Beth had told him, Sophie didn't have a relationship with her parents.

"Thanks for inviting Mom and Dad to the graduation. I know they've been dying to see me ride."

She latched onto the lifeline he threw her. "They need to see you ride. Your brother and sister see it often, and can tell your folks about your progress, but they need to see it for themselves. I've invited the army officers to the ceremony, too. I want them to come out and evaluate the program."

That was the first he'd heard about the army coming to visit. "I hope they plan to spend some time and walk around the ranch and see what you have to offer. Have you submitted the proposal to them?"

"A preliminary one. I need to submit the final draft to them by Monday."

"Would you like for me to look at it? I could glance over it and give you my feedback."

Her shoulders eased and leaned toward him. "That sounds great. You can tell me if I'm missing any of the bells and whistles I need." Her face lit up with excitement.

"Hey, it's the least I can do. I spent enough time in my unit helping others write requests. Our unit commander said I had the gift of *request*. If I requested it, we got it."

That got her attention.

"If that's the case, by all means, come and look my proposal over."

"Since tomorrow is Sunday, would you like to do that

after church? Or I could meet you at church, we could eat afterward, then evaluate the proposal." The words were out of his mouth before he thought.

"I'd like that. I go to New Life Center in south Albuquerque."

"I know where that is." It struck Zach that his church attendance had been sadly lacking. He turned off the main road to the dirt road that led to the ranch.

"Good. There are two services. I usually go to the early service at nine o'clock."

"I can meet you there."

"Wonderful. I really like the pastor. He's an ex-military man. I think you'll like him."

"I'll look forward to it."

He pulled his truck into the parking lot. "Thanks, again, for talking with my parents tonight. I see that they're adapting. They seem to be easier with things."

"True, and it could be you're easier with yourself."

He stopped the truck beside the house. Her words set him back on his heels. Was that what he was feeling tonight? "You think so?"

"It's what you think that's important."

"No, no, don't give me that psychobabble. I was asking your opinion. I got enough of that kinda talk in the hospital."

"I think the reason my answer annoys you is because it's the truth." She put up her hand to stop his objections. "I noticed that your parents did seem easier with you. And the other thing I've noticed is your attitude is different. You don't want to bite anyone's head off."

"I wasn't that bad."

Her brow lifted. "You've changed, Zach. You've been a blessing to me. There's a strength in you that you needed to tap into and you have."

Her words made him realize that he'd come a long way.

"I'll see you tomorrow." She had her hand on the door handle.

He grabbed her wrist, stopping her exit. "I'll walk you to the door."

"That's not necessary, Zach."

Releasing her hand, he turned off the engine. "I know, but my mother taught me manners, Sophie."

Her cheeks puffed out and she blew out air. He easily slipped out of the truck, walked around it and opened the door for her. She shook her head and allowed him to walk her to the door.

She kept her head down as she unlocked the door.

"Sophie."

She looked up. He could see uncertainty in her eyes. He slowly lowered his head, allowing her time to refuse the kiss. She raised her lips fractionally and waited.

Satisfaction unfurled inside him. He cupped her face and covered her mouth with his. He felt her surrender and she returned his kiss. He didn't press for more. Lifting his head, he smiled down at her.

"'Night."

She nodded and slipped inside the door.

As he headed home, Zach felt a hope bubbling up in his spirit. He was looking forward to church tomorrow.

* * *

Sophie sat at the kitchen table, her Bible open, a cup of hot chamomile tea beside the Bible. She couldn't sleep and after an hour of tossing and turning, she got up and brewed some more tea. There were too many thoughts and feelings shooting around inside that she couldn't sort out.

She'd tried talking herself out of what she was feeling, telling herself she was headed for nothing but pain. In college, she liked Zach from afar, never having to engage with him or talk to him. It had been infatuation.

These past few weeks, working side by side with him, she experienced firsthand how after Zach accepted the challenge of building up his strength again, he hadn't turned back. He worked at building up his muscles and stamina.

The kids loved him. Andy couldn't get enough of him, and Zach was like a big brother to all the kids.

He charmed every horse at the ranch.

He won over Ollie.

What chance did she stand against all that charm?

But the cherry on top was seeing how his family loved him and he loved them back. That was how a family should be. Not cold and distant and lost in grief.

Her eyes fell on 2 Corinthians 1:3, 4.

...The God of all comfort, who comforts us in all our troubles, so that we can comfort those in any trouble with the comfort we ourselves have received from God.

Zach could do that.

And she would, too.

Chapter Ten

The final amen resounded through the auditorium. As the last strains of the organ faded, Sophie saw her small group leader, Rita Wells, rush out of the pew across the aisle and hurry over to where Sophie and Zach stood.

"Are you coming to class this morning?" Rita asked, looking at Zach. Sunday School classes ran concurrently with the services. If you went to early service, then you then went to Sunday School afterward and vice versa.

Rita was in her late twenties, the wife of the assistant pastor. She introduced herself before Sophie could open her mouth.

Zach shook Rita's hand.

Rita glanced from Sophie to Zach. "How do you know Sophie?" she asked Zach.

Sophie wanted to grab Zach's arm and rush out of the church before Rita could question him. Rita had a mothering instinct that wanted all the young professionals in the church to find a mate. Sophie had turned down three dates Rita tried to arrange. It wasn't that Sophie didn't appreciate Rita's effort, but Sophie wasn't ready to join the dating scene, even at church.

"Sophie was my sister's roommate in college," Zach explained. "And she is a fellow army vet."

Sophie explained to Rita about their plan for helping soldiers and that's what they were going to do now and why they would be missing class.

The news caught Rita by surprise. She looked from Zach to Sophie, then back again. "I'll be praying for your efforts, Sophie. You let me know if you need any help. I've got a lot of teens who need projects. Your plan for the equine therapy sounds like something we might like to do."

The tension eased from Sophie's shoulders. "Thanks, Rita." She didn't waste any time, but pulled Zach out into the parking lot. They made plans to buy burgers on the way to Sophie's house, then eat them in her kitchen.

Zach picked up the burgers while Sophie went home, changed into jeans and a T-shirt and pulled out drinks and paper plates. Zach arrived a few minutes later and when he walked in, he held up the bags. "Chow."

They eagerly started on the burgers and fries.

"I thought for a minute there after the service that Rita was going to ask me for my ID and see what my intentions were toward you. I wanted to tell her that you're an ex-soldier, and she didn't have to worry about any male's motives because you could take them out."

Sophie choked on her fry. "Why do you say that?"

He sat back in his seat and grinned. "A mama bear isn't as fierce as your Sunday School teacher. I believe she'd be looking out for your interests."

Sophie dipped her fry in the ketchup and popped it into her mouth. "Rita thinks it's part of her job as the wife of the youth pastor to take care of all of us singles. I've been her latest mission." She shrugged. "I can't tell you the number of dates she's tried to set me up with nice guys, but…"

"You go on any of those dates?"

"No."

He rested his elbows on the table and reached for the two-liter bottle of Dr Pepper. "Why not?"

"Because I'm not looking for a boyfriend." She didn't want to tell him that none of those men made her heart flutter like he did. "I've got my hands full with the ranch. I don't have any spare time with trying to get the army program started. Speaking of which—" She stood and walked into the living room where the printer sat. Grabbing the pages from the tray, she brought it back to the table. "Here's my proposal." She handed him the pages. "Tell me what you think." Her stomach clenched with nerves.

Zach took the proposal and began to read it.

Over the next hour, Zach and Sophie went over every page, discussing how to improve and implement the program. He spotted several things he thought to reword, but he was impressed with Sophie's work.

"With those few changes, I think you've got a winner."

"I'll follow up with my army contact, and tell him we've refined the proposal." She smiled and squeezed his hand.

He wanted to lean over and kiss her. He saw the same awareness in her.

"I have some more of those cookies that were in the office." She stood and walked to the counter, grabbed the tin and brought it back to the table. Opening the lid, she presented him with homemade peanut-butter cookies.

"Beth told you that these were my favorite, didn't she?" He grabbed two cookies.

"No, she didn't tell me that. Other secrets, but that wasn't one of them. She told me about you sneaking out with Ethan and both going to a party you were grounded from."

He shrugged. "Well, I've got stories, too. Did Beth tell you that she followed us, then came home and ratted us out to my parents?" He laughed. "I didn't think I'd get to go to my junior prom. Who'd want to go the prom with a guy who had to muck out stalls for a month? I did finally forgive Beth in time for her college graduation," he teased. "But I was disappointed that I didn't see you there after all the work you did to get that degree."

She broke off a piece of the cookie and put it into her mouth. "I needed to report for basic training. You know the army isn't concerned with individual soldiers' time schedules. The drill sergeant didn't care about my walking the stage to receive my diploma. I wasn't going to get a pass."

That was true. You bent around the army, not the other way around. But he knew there were other reasons why she didn't stay. "Why'd you join?"

"I find that question strange coming from a man who joined before I did."

"I joined because both my father and grandfather were in the army. Grandpa, Korea. Dad, Vietnam. It was a McClure thing. And the ranch was going through some tough times and I needed cash to finish school. The army provided it." He popped the rest of the peanut-butter cookie into his mouth.

"The ranch had problems?"

He gave a shout of laughter. "It's only a matter of time before a ranch goes through tough times. When I was a senior in high school, there was a bad drought in the northern part of the state, even for New Mexico. Mom and Dad were already paying for Ethan's college. Don't get me wrong, Ethan worked, tried to pay for as much as he could, but they couldn't swing my college, too. The army was the answer."

She fiddled with the salt and pepper shakers on the table.

"Why'd you join?" Zach pushed.

"I joined for the same reason you did—I needed the money for medical school. I wanted to become a doctor."

Her answer caught him off guard. "So why aren't you in medical school?"

Folding her hands on the table before her, she seemed lost in memories. A bittersweet smile curved her mouth. "I wanted to be a doctor—an E.R. physician—to help save people. But you know how the army changes you. For me, being in the field as medic, I was able to save guys. But I found once I helped save them, they were off on their own." She stopped, staring down at her hands.

"It was equine therapy and the healing that goes on in those sessions that I wanted to do, to help soldiers."

He rested his hand over hers and squeezed.

"It's the best of all worlds, horses and helping others," he supplied.

Her head came up and her gaze locked with his. "You do understand," she said. Her gaze lost focus as if she were remembering something. "My family had horses. My brother Matt loved to ride. So did I. Since we lived in a small town, we kept our horses in the stables outside of town.

"It was a beautiful spring day and we were out on Easter vacation. I'd gotten into trouble. I hadn't done chores around the house and sassed my mom back. I was grounded. I couldn't ride that week. Mom had gone into Albuquerque to buy some new Easter clothes and Dad was off selling insurance. I was feeling persecuted, like only a twelve-year-old girl can feel, and went to the stables. Matt followed. I had saddled my horse, Twinkle, and was on it when Matt found me. He was mad. We argued, and Matt tried to grab Twinkle; she reared. Matt stumbled back and tripped over a pitchfork." She went silent. Tracks of tears ran down her cheeks.

His other hand came up and he held both of her hands.

"One of the tines of the fork pierced his lung and caught his heart. He only lived for about a week after."

Zach saw the horror and guilt in her eyes and he

realized the burning purpose of Sophie's life was to save others when she couldn't save her brother.

"I got to see him in intensive care. He was on a ventilator and couldn't talk. I told him I was so sorry. It was my fault. He shook his head, but I knew it was."

"Sophie."

She refused to look at him.

"Sophie, look at me."

She didn't.

His hand came up and he cupped her chin, raising her gaze to his.

"It was an accident. You didn't intend for your brother to die."

"If I hadn't been at the stables, if I hadn't disobeyed my parents, it wouldn't have happened." Her mouth trembled.

Lord, give me the right words. "Did you want your brother to die?"

She jerked back and glared at him. "Of course not." When she tried to stand to flee, he grabbed her hand.

He stood and pulled her to him. "Did you plan on the event?"

"Are you crazy?"

"It was an accident, Sophie. An awful, tragic accident."

Her eyes sought his, wanting to see the truth of his words.

"You were twelve. Right?"

"Yes."

His hands brushed the hair back from her face. "A twelve-year-old does lots of stupid things, believe me.

You want me to tell you the stupid things I did? That Ethan did? Or Beth? It was an accident, Sophie. There was no malice in your heart."

She collapsed into his chest and wrapped her arms around his waist as the storm of tears broke.

He rubbed her back as her body shook. His heart ached with hers. Her brother's death had scarred her. But with her reaction, he sensed there was more to the story.

He prayed for Sophie's wounded soul and he prayed God would give him the right words to help and comfort her. He now understood the driving force behind this incredible woman.

Finally, she quieted in his arms. She felt so right in his arms.

She hiccupped. A giggle escaped her mouth. She looked up. "Thank you."

"There's nothing to thank me for. I should thank you for kicking me out of my funk."

"It was your family that you should thank. They're the ones who prayed for you."

She stepped out of his embrace, then wiped her face. "I must look a mess." She walked to the kitchen sink, grabbed a paper towel from the roll under the cabinet, and wet it. With both hands, she placed it over her eyes.

He wanted her to talk more about her family, to fill in the part he knew she left out. "You should see Beth when she cries." He shook his head. "It's not pretty."

She laughed. "She might have an ugly cry, but she didn't give up on you."

That brought a grin to his face. "I know. But sometimes family can't get past the obvious. My mother cried every time she looked at my empty pant leg. Dad ignored the situation. Ethan and Beth didn't know whether to beat me or cater to me. How'd your family react?"

Her shoulders hunched. "Not well."

From her tone, he knew she wouldn't say anything more about her brother's death. He wouldn't push.

She picked up the proposal. "I think I'll input these changes and then email it to Colonel Norton. I'll follow up with a call to him tomorrow."

He'd been dismissed. He could fight it, but he wouldn't push. She revealed more of herself than she probably had in years. Beth didn't know the circumstances surrounding Sophie's brother's death. "I'll let myself out. See you tomorrow morning."

She turned and disappeared down the hall. Zach walked out of the house and down the walk. He looked out into the corral behind the stable. Prince Charming and Sam were out. He walked to the fence. When Prince Charming saw him, the horse walked to where he stood.

"Hello, big boy." Zach patted the animal on his neck. "Are you having a fine time for yourself?" The horse nudged his hand.

"I don't have any treats."

Prince Charming stood in front of him. Zach's thoughts returned to Sophie and what she'd revealed. She was twelve when her brother was killed.

That had to have been a dark time for all her family. She still carried open wounds from her brother's death.

Was that why Beth had never seen Sophie's parents visit her at college?

What would it have been like not to have your family surround you and support you?

He'd been around a lot of guys in college and the army who didn't have contact with their families for one reason or another, but he noticed that a break with their families caused a loneliness in that person's heart. Could that be what he saw in Sophie's heart? Loneliness and despair?

He wanted to find out.

Sophie finished typing in the changes that Zach had suggested, saved the file, then composed an email to Colonel Norton. She included a mention of the graduation ceremony that they would have on Wednesday and invited him to come and see what they were doing. She promised to call him tomorrow to confirm plans.

When she hit the send button, she collapsed back into her chair. After exiting her email, Sophie closed her eyes and remembered Zach's words.

It was an accident.

Matt's death was an accident.

How Zach got her to talk about that day, she didn't know. She'd never told anyone about that day. Her parents didn't want to know the details, and her grandmother simply held her and comforted her. She never asked what happened. The only person she told was the sheriff when he came and talked with her. But with Zach the words burst out.

If she hadn't wanted to ride that day…

If Matt hadn't tried to stop her…

If she hadn't sassed her mother…

Matt had finally convinced his parents to allow him to work at the stables at the edge of town to earn extra money caring for other people's horses. Sophie loved to go with Matt and watch him. She often helped with chores. Matt even paid her a couple of dollars from his salary.

She wanted to work there, too. Their mom didn't like Matt working there, thought such manual labor wasn't as dignified as their mother wanted her friends to think of the family of the insurance broker. Having horses was fine and caring for those horses was the right thing, but mucking out stalls for other people wasn't how the privileged did it. But Grandma and their father told Mom she was being ridiculous. And selfish.

Suffocating under the weight of her memories, Sophie walked out of the house to the corral. The horses had been a refuge after Matt's death. Her mother had become withdrawn, seeming to give up. Her father had buried himself in his work, becoming the leading salesman in the Southwest. For Sophie, horses brought her closer to Matt. Neither of her parents objected.

As she walked by the open door of the stables, she heard a man's voice humming.

Drawn by curiosity, she walked into the stables. The tack room door stood open and the hummed tune of "Amazing Grace" drifted out.

She stepped into the door and saw Zach working on bridles. "I thought you went home."

Zach looked up from the leather in his hands. "I

wanted to check the tack before I went home. It gets so busy around here, I thought I might get ahead of the curve."

Nodding, she walked into the room and sat on the barrel beside the door. "I made the changes you suggested and emailed Colonel Norton."

His large hands worked the cloth over the leather.

"It should be an exciting event, the graduation. It's a perfect time to invite people to view the program." He stood and replaced the bridle on the hook on the wall. "It might be a good time to invite your parents to view what you've done."

She jerked as if poked by a stick. "What?"

He moved to her side. "I think your parents would be proud of what you're accomplished here. Just let Andy loose on them. He'll convince them that you are the best thing since sliced bread."

The statement was so over-the-top, she laughed. "You're right. I probably should let Andy loose on the colonel, too."

"Naw, you let me loose on the colonel. I'll convince him that the program will be a benefit for the vets."

"Or I could let Ethan and Beth loose on him."

Zach's laughter echoed in the room. Sophie joined him.

After several minutes, Sophie smiled. "You know what I miss the most about my brother? I miss his laughter. It was a thing of beauty. No matter if you were in a sour mood, Matt's laughter could lift you out of your funk. I know my mother couldn't scold him while she was laughing. Dad loved the laughter. When Matt died, it was as if the light went out of our family."

Zach scooped up her hand. "Your parents were the adults, Sophie."

"You know, Zach, the night Matt died, I went into the living room to tell my mother how sorry I was and I heard her tell Dad if it hadn't been for me, Matt would be alive."

Zach's heart bled. What a devastating thing for a young girl to hear out of her mother's mouth.

"Did you talk to your mother?"

Her gaze fell to their joined hands. "No, I ran back to my room. I couldn't talk to my mother."

"What did your father say?" Maybe it wasn't as bad as it seemed.

Her left shoulder lifted. "I didn't hear what he said. I locked myself in my room. Over the next few days, Mom never said anything to my face, but I saw the accusation in her eyes.

"When we stood over Matt's casket, I wanted to trade places with him." She lifted her head. "I tried to be the best I could, but… My grandmother took up the slack. She tried to comfort me. And my youth pastor was great. He helped me, and got the kids in the church youth group to rally around me. I know I was the subject of a lot of prayers."

He lifted his hand and ran his fingers over her cheek. He wanted to shake Sophie's mother for losing sight of the child she had left. "Perhaps you should try talking to your mother about what happened."

Pulling back she asked, "Why?"

"She might not know you heard. Grief clouded her judgment. It's not fair to hold something a person says when they're mired in grief." He gave her a self-deprecating smile. "I know. I've said some ugly things I had to go back and apologize for. *Repent* is the word your pastor would use. And you're one of the people I have to apologize to."

"You don't have to do that, Zach. I understand the emotional pain you were in."

His eyes locked with hers. He knew when her own words echoed through her heart. She nodded. "I understand your point."

"I knew I was a jerk, Sophie, when you had to come after me that first time, wallowing in self-pity. Maybe your mother doesn't know how she wounded you."

He could see her processing his words. After several long moments, she nodded.

"I see what you're saying. I'll consider it."

He brushed a kiss across her mouth. "You're an amazing woman, Sophie Powell."

"No, I'm not."

He slid his arm around her waist. "Let's go see Prince Charming. I think he might like a carrot."

The lightness of his tone allowed her to relax. "He is rather spoiled."

They walked down the center of the stable to the far barn doors which stood open. Zach grabbed a handful of carrots. Prince Charming and the other horses were out in the corral. Once the horses saw them, Prince Charming made a beeline toward them.

The gelding nodded and bumped Zach's hand.

Sophie laughed. "He's worse than a big puppy."

"He is." Zach fed Prince Charming the carrot.

Sam nudged Sophie. She took a carrot from Zach and fed it to Sam.

"I guess you didn't stop riding after Matt died," Zach said.

Sam munched happily. "It was my way to stay close to Matt. And there were times when I was on a horse that I cried and prayed. God talked to me through the land and horses. I know I talked to Him."

Zach understood that. "Sometimes when I was on my mount, and looked into a sunrise or felt the breeze on my face, I heard the voice of God. There's nothing like it."

"Amen."

That night after Sophie finished her evening chores, she walked into the house realizing that Zach's words had echoed in her spirit all day. They followed her as she fed all the horses. With time and Zach's perspective, she could see her mother's grief had overwhelmed her. Maybe she hadn't wanted Sophie to die, but it had been a wounded heart speaking.

The only way she would know was to talk to them.

Picking up the phone, she dialed her parents' phone number. She ignored the impulse to hang up. On the fourth ring someone picked up.

"Hello."

"Hi, Dad." Her stomach danced with nerves.

"Sophie, this is unexpected."

Not a great starting off point. "I was wondering how you and Mom are doing."

"We're fine. Cindy, pick up the extension," he called out.

Her mother came onto the line. "Hello."

"Hi, Mom." Her stomach jumped with nervousness.

"Sophie."

It wasn't a warm welcome, but Sophie had to admit her part in the rift between them. "I wanted to invite you two to the ranch a week from Wednesday to see what we're doing here. You know I told you about the equine therapy. We're going to have a graduation for the kids. I thought you might like to see what I'm doing."

Both her parents were quiet. Her heart pounded.

"You don't have to come if you don't want," Sophie hurriedly added.

"We'd love to," her father said. "Isn't that so, Cindy?"

"I'd like that."

Sophie's mouth trembled. "Good. I'll see you around two in the afternoon."

"We'll be there," her dad answered.

Sophie next dialed her grandma and asked her to attend the ceremony, too.

"I wouldn't miss it, sugar," her grandmother replied.

"Mom and Dad are going to be there, too," Sophie added.

"It's about time that daughter of mine woke up. Don't you worry your head, Sophie. I'll be nice to your mother."

Sophie had heard her mother and grandmother

arguing several months after her brother's death about her mother ignoring her only living child.

"I know you will be, Grandma. I thought you should know."

"You mean *warn* me. You're a thoughtful child."

When she hung up, hope fluttered in Sophie's heart. A hope she hadn't experienced since Matt's death.

Chapter Eleven

The next week sped by for Sophie. Ollie appeared stronger and was at the ranch every day. Color had returned to his face and his normal reserved attitude came back. Zach's strength also increased each day. By the end of the week, he brought his saber with him to the ranch. He wanted to try the lunge exercise with the "real deal." Zach and Ollie had rigged a hoop in the practice ring before the stands.

Before he started his practice, Zach's parents, brother and sister arrived and scrambled into the bleachers. Apparently, Zach had told his parents what he intended to do. Sophie saw Lynda offer up a prayer.

Zach rode with an ease of a seasoned cowboy and cavalry officer. Sophie smiled with pride. Zach beamed, and Ollie nearly busted his buttons. The McClures went nuts in the stands, with clapping, whistling and stomping on the wooden risers.

"Look at that," Ethan shouted. "Do it again, Zach."

It didn't take any encouraging to get Zach to repeat the performance.

"I knew that boy was good when I first saw him those years ago," Ollie said to Sophie as Zach made another pass at the target. "He's got his balance back."

Joy flooded her. "Alleluia," she whispered, watching the performance. Zach seemed more like the boy she knew those many years ago. He smiled and laughed. He made her heart do somersaults in her chest.

She could only gaze at him in wonder and amazement.

Zach finished his ride. The grin on his face made him look sixteen again. He rode to Ollie's side and handed him his saber and dismounted.

"You're looking good." A smile curved the older man's mouth.

Zach's family raced out of the bleachers.

"Wow," Sophie said, looking at Ollie. Turning, she addressed Zach. "That's some high praise you handed out to him."

Ollie blushed. "I call 'em like I see 'em."

Sophie smiled, wrapping her arm around Ollie's shoulders. "I was teasing."

Before she could add anything, Zach's family engulfed him. Every one of them took turns hugging him.

Sophie's heart ached at the beautiful picture before her. The bridges that had been damaged between parents and child seemed to be repaired.

Lynda scooped Sophie up in a hug. "Thank you for giving me back my son." When Lynda pulled back, her eyes danced with joy.

"I didn't do anything. Zach worked. It's him you need to congratulate. He's done the work."

The chatter had died and Sophie's words rang out. She turned to Zach. "It's true. You worked. It's your victory."

"True, but I had a hard taskmaster."

"Hopefully, the army will share your opinion. I think when those officers come to review the program, you'll blow them away."

The sound of cars pulling up in the parking lot drifted in the air, followed by the sound of car doors slamming.

"I think my time's over," Zach announced. "I'll put Prince Charming away. Sophie, could you lock up my saber in the office?"

His parents left and Sophie took the sword from Ollie. They scattered, each to a different chore.

An hour later, after Andy's session, his mother arrived to pick him up. Sophie had to take a call in the office. After she finished, she went looking for Zach. She needed to huddle with him about the call she had just received from the colonel.

When Sophie walked into the stables, she heard Andy ask, "So how do you keep that fake foot on?"

"It's a neat way. A vacuum."

"You mean like my mom's? That machine she uses to clean the carpet?"

Sophie stopped, curious to see what Zach would say.

"It's like that in a way. My fake leg latches onto my real leg. Ever put your hand under the vacuum?"

She couldn't see Andy, but she could imagine his expression.

"My leg's the same. See this button?"

"Yeah."

"If you press it, it makes the fake leg let go of my real leg."

Sophie peered around the corner to see Andy's little head bent over Zach's leg.

"Can I press it?" Andy looked up. His mother stood behind Andy.

Zach looked at his mother. She nodded.

"Sure."

The little boy pressed the button and the artificial leg slipped off.

"Oh, that's cool. It'd be fun if I had one of those."

"It's nice I have this leg, but it would be easier if I had my real leg, like you. This—" he said, touching the artificial limb "—makes things harder."

"So why'd you get this if you liked your real leg."

Andy's mom's eyes widened.

Zach put up his hand. "It was an accident when I was a soldier. But the doctors fixed me up. And that's why I've been riding, to help me."

Andy sat back on his haunches. "I'm sorry for your accident. But it's good you have that 'ficial leg. You can walk normal."

"That's true." Zach slipped his leg back into the prosthesis.

Sophie walked around the corner.

Andy glanced up. "You see Zach's leg? I've been

asking him if I could see. He talked to my mama and she said it was 'kay."

Andy jumped to his feet. "I understand now why he had to have the 'ficial leg. I wanted one, but it's good I have my own real legs." He smiled at his mom. "Let's go. I can't wait to tell Dad about this."

Andy's mom stepped to Zach's side. "Thank you. He's been curious about why you had the leg, why he couldn't have one, too, and why you got it."

Zach shrugged. "It's not a problem. And I think I answered his questions."

She nodded and went after her son. She paused by Sophie. "I hope you don't mind that Andy wanted to see Zach's leg."

Still struggling for her emotional balance, Sophie smiled. "Of course not. I'm glad that Zach could answer Andy's questions."

"Mom," Andy yelled.

"I'm coming," she replied. "Thank you." She nodded toward Zach.

Sophie leaned against the hall wall. Bewildered, she didn't know what to say.

"You upset?" Zach asked. He watched her carefully, expecting—what? Anger? Reprimand?

"No. I'm not upset. Surprised, but not upset."

"Are you going to yell at me that I shouldn't have showed Andy my leg."

She didn't know where he was going. "No. If Andy's mom talked to you about the situation, I'm okay with it. Were you okay with it?"

He readjusted the cushioning sock on his stump and

then put his leg into the prosthesis. He stood, putting pressure on the leg. He then pushed his pant leg down over the leg. The low boots he wore had a lower heel than normal cowboy boots, but when his pant leg fell over the boot, she couldn't tell that his shoes were anything else but a true cowboy boot.

"She surprised me, but she told me of how Andy wanted a 'ficial leg, too, just like Zach. I think she wanted to die of embarrassment, but Andy wanted to see my leg." He shrugged. "Andy asked honestly, so I showed him."

She noted how carefully he watched her reaction.

"You handled it perfectly. Thanks for answering his questions."

He visibly relaxed as if he'd been expecting a stern lecture.

"I was coming to tell you that I got a call from the colonel just a few minutes ago. He's bringing his team out next Monday to look over the ranch and talk to us."

"That's great news. I'll be sure to be here bright and early." He started down the center aisle of the stables. He stopped and turned. "You like country music?"

"Yes."

"I have tickets for a Reba McEntire and Tim McGraw concert in Santa Fe this Friday night. Would you like to go?"

Suddenly, Sophie felt sixteen and being asked out on her first date.

"We could do dinner and the show."

"What about the horses?"

Laughing, he quipped, "I don't have tickets for them."

Resting her hands on her hips, she glared at him.

"I'll get Ethan to come and help us settle the stock. Will that do?"

"It will. And yes, I'd love to go with you to the concert."

"It's a date." He turned and walked away, whistling.

Turning, Sophie came face-to-face with Ollie. He grinned. "Good choice."

Smiling, she shook her head. If she didn't know better, she'd have thought Ollie set up the whole deal.

After the last rider's mother picked her up, the volunteers and sidewalkers helped care for the horses, bedding them down for the night. Ollie and Zach worked along with the volunteers.

As Sophie put out hay, she heard Austin in the stables. "As you can see, the stable is in great shape. If you want, you could also buy the stock, too."

Sophie froze in the stall.

"I'd like to look at the horses you have."

Sophie walked out of the stall. Zach emerged from the tack room. Ollie walked in from the large open doors at the end of the stables.

Austin and the man with him stopped.

"What can I do for you, Austin?" Sophie asked. She felt Zach's and Ollie's support.

He glanced at Zach, then back over his shoulder at

Ollie. "Nothing. I was showing Mr. Jamison around the ranch."

The man held out his hand. "Cole Jamison."

Sophie shook his hand. "Sophie Powell. I'm in charge of running the ranch until Margaret returns."

Jamison's brow shot up. "I thought you told me that your mother was selling the ranch."

Both Zach and Ollie straightened.

With a tight smile, Austin nodded. "Mother realizes she's not ever going to be able to return to the day-to-day running of the ranch and decided to sell it."

Zach moved behind her. Ollie stepped forward.

"When did she tell you that, Austin?" Sophie calmly asked.

Glaring daggers at her, he said, "I'll talk with you later, Ms. Powell, after I've finished giving Mr. Jamison his tour." With those words, Austin dismissed her and guided Mr. Jamison out of the stable.

Sophie drew in several deep breaths to prevent herself from running after Austin and saying something she would later regret.

"Who was that?" Zach's words came from behind her.

"That was Margaret's son."

"And he wants to sell the ranch?"

She spun and looked up at him. "That's what it appears to be."

"Doesn't he know about the program you're developing for the army? And what of his mother's wishes."

"It won't matter to him," Ollie spat out. "He's a little worm. He's never wanted any of this. He didn't support the equine-therapy program. I heard him arguing with his mother about this. Margaret did it in spite of her son's opposition."

Zach sat on the barrel outside one of the stalls. "What does this do to our plans for the army?"

"Nothing," Sophie answered.

Both men looked at her.

"When Margaret and I decided to try to set up this program for the vets, Margaret realized that if something happened to her, she told me I had first right to buy this ranch."

Ollie grinned. "Ah, that's my Margaret."

Sophie hid her shock at Ollie's comment. Ollie and Margaret?

Zach stood. "If Margaret wanted to sell, could you buy the ranch?"

"Yes, I have that right, and I'm sure Austin doesn't know about that."

Ollie slapped his leg as a bark of laughter escaped. "It'll be a major sticking point to his plan to get rid of this place."

"Did you put it in writing?" Zach asked.

"Yes."

Zach's eyes crinkled at the corners as he grinned. "Aw, you're a smart girl."

"Well, I have to share that title with Margaret. We decided to put our agreement in writing, just in case something happened. And it did."

Sophie walked out of the stable and watched as Austin and Jamison walked to their cars. Sophie waved at Austin. "I need to talk to you," she called out.

Austin said something to the other man, and slapped him on the shoulder. Jamison got in his car and drove off. Austin waited until the other man was out of the parking lot before he walked toward Sophie.

"What can I do for you, Ms. Powell?

"How's your mother?" Sophie asked.

"She's improving. Her speech is getting better. The doctors tell us they don't think she'll walk again. She won't ever be able to run a ranch again."

Hearing how poorly Margaret was doing, Sophie wanted to cry. "I'm sorry to hear that, but I do have to tell you that your mother gave me first right to buy this ranch."

Austin's dismissive attitude evaporated. "What?"

"Your mom told me if she decided to sell this ranch, I would have the first right to buy this place."

"I know nothing of this."

"Your mother conducted business and I'm sure you didn't know of most of the day-to-day items of business she dealt with."

He waved off her words. "You could say anything you like and it doesn't make it true."

"You're right, but we put our agreement in writing."

His eyes widened. "I'd like to see that."

"I'll find that agreement and I can fax you a copy of it. I also think that she left a copy of the agreement with her lawyer. He'll have a copy of it, too."

"I'll check out your story. I'll be back in contact with you." With those final chilly words, he stalked to his car, got in it and sped off.

Later that night, after Sophie faxed a copy of the agreement to Austin, she got a call from him.

"You've got until next Friday to come up with the money for the ranch." He named a sum.

"That is not fair market value," Sophie replied. "Did your mother okay that?"

"I've been appointed guardian over the estate. That's the price I want for the ranch."

Sophie heard what he left unsaid. That was the price that Jamison would pay.

"If you can't come up with the sum, I'll sell it to another bidder." He hung up.

Sophie stared at the phone as if it was a snake. What was she going to do? She thought she knew what God wanted her to do, run this ranch. Help others.

"Lord, with You everything is possible. I need Your help now."

Chapter Twelve

Sophie left the bank and walked to her truck. The loan application seemed to go smoothly. The bank wanted collateral. The contract with the army would provide that. The loan officer knew Margaret and her, and was reassured by the future income.

Thinking of her old friend, Sophie wanted to see Margaret, to touch base with her.

The private recovery hospital was near the bank. It took only a few minutes to drive to the facility. Margaret had come back from her physical-therapy session. When the attendant wheeled her into the room, Sophie noticed a sparkle in the older woman's eyes.

The man left Margaret in the wheelchair.

Sophie kissed Margaret on the cheek. "How are you doing?"

Margaret nodded. Speech was still hard for her.

Sophie pulled her chair next to Margaret and took her hand. "We miss you at the ranch, but the Lord sent Zach McClure." Sophie spent the next twenty minutes talking about what had happened at the ranch, how Zach came to the ranch and her deal with him.

"I think those army officials will be blown away with what we can do. You should see him, Margaret. He's physically stronger, but I see a smile on his face. And laughter. He started laughing again.

"I nearly passed out when I saw Zach showing Andy his prosthesis." She shook her head, a grin playing on her mouth. "But that action answered all of Andy's questions. Zach has a wonderful way with the kids." Looking down at Margaret's hands, she whispered, "I'm confused, old friend." She raised her head. "I think I'm falling in love. But I'm scared, Margaret."

"No," the older woman said.

"No, what?"

"Afraid. Trust—" She tapped her heart.

Sophie didn't know if she could trust her heart. "That's easier said than done."

Margaret squeezed her hand. "Ranch. Heard Austin sell."

Sophie wondered if Margaret knew about her son's actions. "Do you want to sell the ranch?"

The door to the room opened and Austin stood there.

"What are you doing here?" he demanded in his usual nasty tone.

Sophie leaned back in her seat. She wondered if Austin paid someone to report her appearances to him. "I came to see your mother. She's making good progress."

"She is, and she probably needs to rest now after her session."

Margaret shook her head. "Stop."

Austin came to her side. "Mother, you need your rest."

Sophie didn't want to upset her old friend or bring any more problems into the situation.

"I need to go." Sophie patted Margaret's hand. "You're looking good and you're in my prayers."

Margaret tried to smile, but her weak left side gave her smile a lopsided twist.

Sophie quickly left the room and started down the hall. Standing in front of the elevator doors, Sophie noticed Austin walking out of his mother's room toward her. He held up his hand, preventing her from getting on the elevator when the doors opened.

"Ms. Powell, I don't want you visiting my mother without me in the room." Hostility radiated off the man as heat came off the stove.

"Why is that?"

"Because I don't want you to say things that will upset her," he responded.

"Like the truth?"

"Maybe your version of the truth."

"Too late. She knows you want to sell the ranch."

Austin's lips compressed. "I don't want you around my mother."

"Why, Austin? Margaret and I are friends. We've been friends for a long time, since before I graduated from high school."

He stepped closer. "I know, and you've been trying

to worm your way into her heart from the first. What's wrong with your relationship with your own mother that you have to find another?"

Sophie gasped.

The second elevator doors pinged opened and Ollie walked out. He looked at the two before him.

"Everything okay?" Ollie asked.

Sophie turned to her friend. "Yes. Margaret's doing well."

Ollie nodded, but he didn't move.

She walked into the elevator. As the door slid closed, she saw Austin glaring at her.

Zach parked his truck beside the guesthouse on the ranch. He felt like a raw sixteen-year-old on his first date. Things were moving so fast, he needed to hold on or he was going to be thrown off this pony.

He finally acknowledged his feelings for Sophie. If he was honest with himself, he'd had feelings for her for a long time. She was amazing. Watching all the people depending on her, he knew that she didn't shirk from any of the responsibilities.

But he knew she had a hole in her heart. He understood that. She had wounds. He did, too.

He knocked on her door.

"It's open," she called out.

He walked into the living room. He felt foolish for bringing her flowers, but if this was an official date, he wanted to do it right. He looked down on his clean, white Western shirt and his starched jeans. The creases were military sharp. He had on his winning buckle. It wasn't the "all-around" that he wanted, but it reflected his wins.

He tested his new boots. He'd talked to the army to see if he could get another prosthesis that he could put into a boot. Once that prosthesis was slipped into the flat of the boot, it would be next to impossible to get out, but it was worth it to be wearing real Western boots again. He had on his best Stetson, but took it off inside.

He heard a sound from the hall and turned. The breath left his chest. Sophie stood there in a peasant blouse and a tiered white skirt. A silver concha belt circled her small waist and a beautiful squash blossom silver necklace hung around her neck. On her left wrist she wore an engraved silver cuff bracelet.

Her long hair fell loose down her back and silver earrings dangled among the strands of reddish brown hair.

His mouth fell open.

She gave him a shy smile. "Too much?"

Words stuck in his throat. It was like Prince Charming kicked him in the chest.

"I thought I'd get in the spirit of the concert and go Western, but if it's too much—" She started to turn.

"No." His brain finally kicked into gear. "It's not too much." Swallowing, he stepped forward. "Don't change. You look great."

The blush on her cheeks faded. Her gaze ran over him from head to toe. "Apparently, I'm not the only one who got dressed up."

He grinned. "Yup. I decided to do it up good. It reminds me of my first dress-up dance. My jeans had so much starch they stood on their own."

Her laugh touched his heart.

"I'm surprised those jeans didn't crack when I sat in my truck to pick up my date." He looked down at the jeans he had on now. "These aren't that bad. Of course, my uniforms had their share of starch." He knew she'd understand that comparison.

He realized he still held the daisies and tiger lilies. Raising his hand, he offered them to her. When she smiled, Zach noticed a dimple on the right side of her mouth.

"Thank you."

Their hands touched and the electricity ran up his arm. She moved away and went into the kitchen. After opening several cabinets, she pulled out a tall plastic cup. "This will have to do. I'm sure Margaret has something up in the main house, but I don't think I'll find anything here in the guesthouse."

After fixing the flowers, she put them on the table.

"Let me get my purse and wrap and we can go."

She disappeared into the other room.

Suddenly, life was very sweet. *Thank You, Lord. I know my attitude stank, but You were there and didn't leave me to my own pity.*

Sophie appeared, a gold shawl covering her shoulders. "I'm ready."

"Then let's go and stomp our feet."

The concert had been great. Sophie hummed the last duet Reba and Tim sang. Zach joined in. His wonderful baritone filled the cab of the truck.

"I think you went into the wrong business," Sophie said after they finished.

"Naw, I wasn't interested in singing." He shot a glance at her. "But the choir director nabbed me when my voice changed. Of course, he had to wait because one day I could sing the notes and the next day, I could've been a tenor. I'm telling you, there's nothing worse than trying to be cool in front of all the girls at school and church and then having my voice be all over the map."

"Well, that's a good reason, but your voice changed a long time ago. I think your excuse has run its course."

"Ya think?"

She laughed. "It's a convenient excuse."

He pulled into the parking lot of a trendy restaurant that claimed to serve home cooking and old-fashioned fare like your grandma cooked. It stood on the corner of a square filled with restaurants, trendy shops and several coffeehouses.

Studying the restaurant, she said, "I've wanted to try the food here. I heard good things about it." The fantasy night continued. She waited for Zach to come around and open the door for her. She got out and waited for Zach to close the door. Zach slipped his arm through hers as he guided her inside.

They were quickly seated and continued to joke and tease during dinner. Once outside, Zach guided her past his truck to a trendy new coffeehouse down the street. Over their lattes and cappuccinos Zach asked about the loan and status of the army proposal.

"I think the bank was impressed that I could get that contract. I touched base with the colonel yesterday and everything's a go. But I wouldn't be surprised if they just show up another day. You know, one of those surprise inspections." She saw the understanding in his eyes.

"I've been there and I know the drill. I remember one day—"

"Zach," a booming voice called out. A tall man approached the small table. "It's so good to see you."

Zach stood and shook the man's hand. "Tyler. What are you doing here?"

The man stepped back and nodded to Sophie. He turned back to Zach. "I'm out. My unit came back to the States around Christmas."

Zach turned to Sophie. "This is Tyler Lynch. He was with a unit in northern Iraq. Our paths crossed when he was briefly assigned to my unit to see how to operate some new equipment we got from the States." He introduced Sophie and bragged on her service.

Tyler's attitude changed and the walls he'd put up seemed to lower. She was a vet and he knew he could talk freely.

"Sit," Zach said.

Tyler waited for Sophie to okay the invite.

"Please join us."

The woman working behind the counter shouted a "Café Americano." Tyler jumped up and got his coffee. He rejoined them. "I missed this when I was in Iraq."

He sat and they quickly began to swap stories.

"So you were a medic?" Tyler asked.

"I was. Unfortunately, I saw more than my share of the war."

Tyler looked down at the tablecloth. "My unit

adopted a stray puppy while we were there. We called him Dodger, because we found her under a piece of a blown-up car. I guess she was far enough from the explosion that the piece of fender knocked her out. I heard a whimper and thought we might have a child. Searching through the rumble, we found her. Our medic cleaned up the wounds on her side and she stayed in our tent until she was well."

His story touched Sophie's heart. She rested her right arm on the table. "What happened to Dodger?"

"I had to go through a lot of channels, but I brought her home with me."

Sophie clapped and met Zach's smiling eyes.

"Too bad you couldn't have taken your horse," Sophie teased.

Tyler looked from her to Zach. "Am I missing something?"

Zach explained what had happened to him.

"Man, I'm sorry to hear that." Tyler looked over Zach. "I never would've guessed it the way you walked across the floor and shook my hand."

"I think you're going to have to thank Sophie. She's the hard drill sergeant who whipped me into shape."

Tyler's body language changed and he focused his attention on Sophie. "Tell me about it."

They spent the next forty-five minutes talking to Tyler about what they wanted to do at the ranch.

"If you'd like, come to the ranch," Sophie offered, seeing the man's interest. "If you live close, we always need sidewalkers. Also, we have a little graduation on

Wednesday for the kids in the program. You might enjoy seeing that."

"I might check that out." He stood. "It was nice meeting you, Sophie." Holding out his hand, he turned to Zach.

Zach grabbed Tyler's hand and stepped forward. With a slap on the back, he whispered something in Tyler's ear.

Sophie watched as Tyler threaded his way through the crowd and out the door. Zach sat down.

Toying with her paper cup, Sophie murmured, "I wonder what memories he's wrestling with."

"You saw that darkness in his eyes, too."

"Yes." Sophie's mind filled with her own visions of war—wounded men and women, blood, missing limbs, the cries of the wounded, the silent haunted eyes. The silent ones were the worst. She recognized that look anywhere. "What'd you say to him?"

Zach hesitated, then said, "I told him he wasn't alone."

"You think working with the horses might help him?"

"You've made a believer out of me. I think it will help him." His forehead wrinkled. "I found it interesting that he brought the dog back with him from Iraq."

They exited the shop and strolled back to his truck. His fingers tucked a long strand of hair behind her ear. "You're amazing, Sophie Powell."

"Why do you say that?"

His lips tilted up at one corner. "Because you're ready to jump headlong into helping Tyler."

She slid into the truck. Zach closed the door and walked around the front and got into the driver's seat. As he pulled out into traffic, he glanced at her. "Nothing to say?"

"There's nothing to say. I recognize pain and want to help."

He fell silent as he drove her back home. She stewed over Zach's words. She recognized pain. It was an area she knew a lot about.

As he parked his truck beside her house, he grabbed her hand and brought it to his lips. "I didn't mean to make you uncomfortable."

"You didn't."

He nodded and released her hand. Sophie didn't wait for him to open her door. She slipped out of the truck and met him on the walk to the house.

He took her hand again and walked with her to the porch. "Talking with Tyler tonight, I saw his hurting and guilt."

She jerked around to face him. "Guilt?"

"Yeah, I saw it." He touched his chest. "I've also felt my own guilt."

What was he talking about?

"Guilt for living when others didn't," he explained. "I should've done a better job on that last patrol. When I was telling you you needed to forgive yourself for your brother's death, I had the head knowledge.

"Seeing Tyler tonight, I realize that those words have to be more than something I throw out. I have to do it. I have to forgive myself." There was no joy in his smile, only sadness and pain. "Sophie, you need to cut yourself some slack. Forgive yourself."

Her heart pounding, she whispered, "It can't be that easy."

"You're wrong. When a person gets saved, that's the argument they use. It can't be that easy. It is." He grabbed her other hand and held it close to his chest. "Lord, help Sophie and me to forgive ourselves. You've forgiven us, now show us how easy it is. Amen."

When her eyes met his, she knew every word out of Zach's mouth was truth.

He kissed her forehead. "I'll talk to you tomorrow."

She watched him leave. On unsteady legs, she walked to the barn. Sam bobbed her head, drawing Sophie to her side.

"Is it that easy, Sam?" Sophie rubbed the white blaze on her nose. Closing her eyes, she whispered, "Lord, I give You the guilt I've been carrying. You forgave me, and I forgive myself."

Suddenly, Sophie felt a peace in her soul. The weight of guilt pressing on her heart wasn't there.

She opened her eyes and looked around, expecting a two-ton stone somewhere on the floor behind her. Everything was as it had been before, and yet the barn looked brighter. Sharper. More full of life.

Sam nodded her head.

"So you're agreeing with me that burden is gone?"

Sam butted her. Sophie held the mare's head and kissed her as tears slid down Sophie's cheeks.

Her steps back to the house were lighter. The world was new.

* * *

Zach woke early and ate, and read his Bible. He couldn't wait for church. Last night when he heard himself comforting Sophie, the words that tumbled out of his mouth shocked him. Every word he uttered was directed at himself.

He knew he'd been holding on to guilt. Last night, he gave that burden away. He'd tried to protect his men. He'd sensed the danger and tried to short-circuit it.

Always, he would grieve his friends' death, but peace had settled in his spirit.

Glancing down at the table, he saw the verse in Joshua 22:3, 4 and it resonated in his heart.

For a long time now—to this very day—you have not deserted your brothers, but have carried out the mission the Lord your God gave you...now return to your homes....

He hadn't deserted his men and tried to save them all. Most of his men came home. He gave it his all and reading those verses gave him peace. "Lord, thank You for taking that burden from me and giving me a pardon."

His guilt was forgiven. It was no longer his.

He got it and he was ready to go to church and celebrate.

Chapter Thirteen

At nine in the morning on Monday, Colonel Norton arrived with two other officers. He introduced the two men with him, Major Simms and Captain Perry. All three men were with the Cavalry and out of Fort Sam Houston in San Antonio.

"I'm glad we finally meet face-to-face, Captain Perry," Sophie told him. "Your suggestions for therapy were excellent. And Zach here is living proof."

After introductions were made, Zach told the officers his story and showed them his leg. He then brought Prince Charming out of his stall, saddled him with a regular saddle and mounted the horse.

Sophie held back the tears of pride, knowing she didn't want to be seen as an emotional female in front of these men. She wanted their respect. Later, she'd have a good cry and offer her prayers of thanks to the Lord.

Zach went through several of the exercises he used. When he did his saber lunges, Sophie knew he impressed the captain.

"Attaboy," Ollie said under his breath as Zach rode around the ring again for another jab.

Sophie's eyes never left the Colonel and Major. Their expressions gave away none of their thoughts.

The sound of a car arriving floated in the air. A door slammed, followed by Andy's mom yelling, "Walk, son, don't run."

"Aw, Mom."

Zach made one more pass at the target.

"Wow," Andy cried. He ran to Sophie. "Did you see that?" As he walked to the corral fence, he said to Zach, "You're getting real good."

Zach stopped Prince Charming beside Andy. "I've been practicing."

"Me, too. I'm better, too."

Zach rested his forearm on the saddle horn. "You are, and there are some people here who'd like to see you ride."

Andy glanced at the officers sitting in the bleachers. "They have on fancy uniforms."

Sophie bit back her smile. "Okay, Andy, let's get you ready to ride."

The boy grinned.

The officers spent the day watching how things were handled. At one point, when a sidewalker didn't make it, the major took off his uniform coat and worked beside Zach. All three men were comfortable around horses and did their share. They talked to the parents and riders. Once during the day, Sophie saw Ollie bending the ear of the major.

At the close of the day, Sophie sat in the office and faced the men.

"Do you have any further questions for me?" she asked.

Major Simms studied her. "Do you plan on having a therapist here on site?"

"I work in tandem with most of the kids' doctors and if they have therapists, I keep in contact with them."

"You realize that the men you'll be dealing with will need to have a therapist on site."

Her stomach twisted into a knot. "That could be arranged."

Colonel Norton's laserlike eyes pinned her. "Are you the owner of the ranch?"

"Margaret Stillwell owns the ranch at the moment, but I'm in the process of buying it."

"Is the owner about?" he pressed.

Sophie felt Zach stiffen beside her. "No. Margaret had a stroke and that's why she needs to sell the ranch. But when we came up with this proposal, Margaret was healthy and wanted to expand the program to help vets. Zach is a perfect example of how horses can bridge a gap in therapy that sometimes a skilled therapist has difficulty."

The men looked at Zach.

"You've seen my leg. I fell flat on my face walking around the ring the first time. But the lure of riding again and being with horses was stronger than my pride."

"But you were raised around horses," Captain Perry countered.

"I was, but there's magic in a horse and each of you know that, being horse people. It's a win-win for the soldier."

"It really doesn't matter," Sophie added. "When I was in D.C. attending a workshop, I went out to the program that worked with the caisson horses used at Arlington National Cemetery. Some of the soldiers didn't have any experience with horses. Others did, but it didn't matter. It's how the patient feels on top of that magnificent animal. They're connected. They feel as if they have their power back. It helped every patient I saw. Double amputees, single, even one man who lost both legs and an arm."

The three officers sat back. Colonel Norton looked at his watch. "We've got a plane to catch." He rose and the others followed. "Thank you for letting us see the facility. We'll be in contact."

Sophie accompanied the officers to their car. As she watched them drive away, Zach rested his hand on her shoulder.

"Don't worry about it."

She turned to him. "How can I not? I think things went well until they asked about a therapist."

"That's something you can get." He pulled her into his arms.

"I hope you're right."

Laughter rumbled through his chest. "I am. Ask Beth and Ethan. I'm always right."

She raised her head. "Is that so?"

A self-satisfied smile curved his mouth. "It is."

* * *

Wednesday dawned bright and clear. Sophie's stomach jumped and twisted as if she'd swallowed a mouthful of grasshoppers. She walked to the refrigerator, grabbed the whole milk and poured herself a glass. When she was a kid, her mother would pour her a glass of milk and tell her milk was magic and would fix anything.

The milk was from the local dairy the next ranch over. The rich taste made Sophie smile. She drank the glass. Her stomach settled. "I hope you're here today, Mom. If you are, I'll have to thank you."

Sophie sat down at the kitchen table, opened her Bible and spent several minutes reading. She closed her Bible and bowed her head and prayed. "Lord, help us today. Let me walk with Your wisdom, because I know I'll need it."

Sitting back, she opened her eyes. It was time to face the day.

Zach looked out from the stable entrance to the stands, which were filled with parents—the riders' parents and his parents. He saw a couple come and talk to Sophie, then an elderly lady. Sophie hugged and kissed the old lady. By the time he got to her side, the group was gone. "Who was that?" he asked.

"My parents and grandmother."

His gaze snapped back to hers. "Your parents?"

A frown settled between her eyes. "You think I don't have parents?"

He realized his mistake too late. "No. I just haven't met them."

Her expression remained firm, then a smile broke across her face. "You know, you look kinda cute when you blush."

This conversation was a losing proposition for him. "I need to make sure all the horses are ready."

Her laughter followed him into the interior of the stable. As he walked to Prince Charming's stall, his mind went over the meeting he saw. Sophie politely greeted her parents, but she hugged her grandmother with an openness. That made sense from what she'd told him and what his sister said.

He quickly saddled Prince Charming and led the horse outside. Sophie stood in front of him directing the other volunteers.

"Are we ready?" Zach asked.

She didn't turn. "I think so. You want to take the riders down the path to the river?"

"You think the kids will make it that far?"

Glancing back over her shoulder, she said, "Yes."

They would do the graduation in two waves. There weren't enough horses to let all the kids ride at once. Also the volunteers would come in two waves.

Zach mounted Prince Charming. Every time he put his foot into the stirrup and hoisted himself into the saddle, he offered a prayer of thanks. He didn't think he'd ever take for granted being able to ride.

From his perch on top of Prince Charming, he saw Tyler, his army buddy from Iraq, in the audience. By his side sat a black dog. A mutt. The dog sat quietly, not being disturbed by the crowd. "Tyler's here."

Sophie looked into the audience. "I see him. And he has a dog?"

"Remember he told us about that dog."

"Yeah, I remember. Okay, let's go." Sophie walked to the mounting block. Andy scrambled up on Sam.

It took several minutes for the rest of the riders to mount, their sidewalkers beside each horse.

Sophie led Sam out into the ring. "I want to thank everyone for coming today. Each of the riders you see here has worked hard and improved their balance and strength. I want to thank the parents here today for working with us."

"Hey, Mom," Andy said, waving to his mother.

The crowd laughed.

"We're going to ride around the ring and then take the path to the pond beyond the last corral. You are welcome to walk down there with us, but if you don't want to walk down there, you're welcome to stay here."

Zach rode out and Sophie followed, leading Sam. All the other horses fell in line behind them. Zach rode out of the corral and started down the path. Pictures were snapped and parents called out to their children.

It was better than any championship rodeo buckle he could earn, Zach thought. And suddenly Zach knew God had shown him the new path his life was to take.

People milled about the tables set up under the trees at the far side of the rings. Several mothers had baked cookies and cupcakes. Ollie had brought a case of soft drinks. Andy's mom had a bowl of punch for the kids.

"Did you see me, Mom?" one of the little girls asked.

"I was good—"

"What a good job you did—"

Voices floated around Sophie. All the snatches of conversation she heard were positive.

Sophie's parents stopped before her.

"This is impressive," her dad said, looking around at the crowd. "You did this yourself?"

"No. Margaret and I worked together."

"Where is she?" her mother asked.

"Stop, Cindy," Sophie's grandmother scolded. "Don't you have anything nice to say to your daughter?"

Her mother's spine stiffened.

"Margaret had a stroke," Sophie quickly supplied, hoping to defuse the tension. "She's recovering. Weren't the kids great?"

"I was amazed," her grandmother said. "They all looked like they were enjoying themselves."

"Miss Sophie," Andy called out, running to her side. "You see my mom and grandma waving at me? And Zach's parents? I told them not to worry about Zach's leg. It worked fine."

Sophie ruffled Andy's hair. He turned and looked up.

"You know Miss Sophie?"

Sophie's father nodded. "I do. She's my daughter."

Pride laced her father's words. Sophie bit her lips to keep them from quivering.

"Really?" Andy looked from her father to Sophie.

"Yes. And this is Sophie's mother and grand-mother."

Andy smiled at each woman. "Are you as proud of Miss Sophie as my mom is of me?"

"Andy, Andy," his mother called.

He ducked his head. "I gotta go." He waved and dashed off.

Sophie noticed that her parents didn't answer Andy's questions, but silence reigned.

Finally, her mother cleared her throat. "You have a lot of volunteers here."

"I do. I've been amazed by the number of people who donate their time to help with the kids. If I get the army contract, I know I'll have plenty of ex-military members who will help. And wasn't Zach amazing? He's Beth's brother."

Her father glanced over at Zach, who huddled with his family. "I don't understand. He rode at the front of the line."

"Dad, he was wounded in Iraq and lost the lower half of his right leg."

"Oh."

"Zach was my test case."

"I heard my name being used." Zach strode up to the group. His family surrounded him.

Sophie did the introductions. Sophie stepped back and listened in amazement as Zach's family sung her praises.

"It is amazing what she's done with Zach," Lynda gushed.

Sophie watched her parents' reaction to the McClures'

praise and their glowing opinions of the work done at the ranch. Andy's praise, combined with the McClures', made her mother squirm. Her grandma caught Sophie's eye and winked.

One of the mothers pulled Sophie away from her family. That was the last time she was able to talk to them. Other people demanded her time. The volunteers and families thanked her.

She watched Zach talk to the veteran they'd met the other night. The dog beside him sat quietly. The dog's eyes moved over the crowd, but he didn't leave his master's side. No leash kept the dog in place. Sophie wanted to join the conversation, but knew Zach and Tyler needed time to talk.

"Guide Zach's words, Lord," she whispered. Although Tyler had all his limbs, he wasn't whole. There were wounds in his spirit that needed healing. That's what she wanted to do, help the healing.

She might be in this place because of the guilt she'd carried from her youth, but freed from that weight, Sophie discovered this is what she wanted to do. She had a talent and a love for this work.

Late in the afternoon after all the families had cleared out, and her parents and Zach's parents had left, Sophie looked out at the empty yard.

"I think your graduation succeeded beyond your wildest dreams."

When Sophie turned, she saw the slight limp in Zach's gait. "You're tired."

"So are you."

"It's a good tired. Kinda like Moses at the end of

that battle with—oh, some guys—the Israelites were still wandering around the desert. They were attacked and as long as Moses had his arms raised the Israelites were winning. When he put his arms down, they were losing. As I recall, he had to have assistance holding up his arms."

"I know the feeling. C'mon, I'll walk you back to the house then head on out."

"I wish Colonel Norton could've seen this."

Zach shrugged. "You know the army. They work on their schedule, but at least they made it here."

He slipped his arm around her shoulders. She felt his unsteady gait. As they reached the front walk of the house, a car pulled up. Austin got out. Over the years, Sophie watched Austin go from a tall, thin man to a man with a beer belly and a constant frown.

"You got the money for the ranch, Sophie?"

Not so much as *a hello, how are you, Mom's doing better,* but rather *you got the money?* "No. My loan hasn't come through yet. The army was here on Monday. We should have an answer any day."

"You've got until Friday or I'll assume you're not interested and I'll accept the other bid on the property."

"But—"

"I've honored your agreement with Mother. You've been given first opportunity. If you don't meet the deadline, it's not my fault." He got back into his car and drove away.

"Is that man always that abrasive?"

Sophie frowned. "I'm not the best judge of character when it comes to Austin. I know he's never liked this ranch and never felt comfortable here. I'm sure it's not a hard thing for him to sell this place."

They walked into the house.

"Sit and I'll get us something to drink."

Zach collapsed onto the sofa.

In the kitchen, Sophie poured them large glasses of iced tea. She needed to call the bank and check the status of the loan. Austin wanted this to be over.

Carrying the glasses of tea back into the living room, the blinking light on the answering machine caught her eye.

She handed Zach his tea and walked to the answering machine.

"Let me check this. It might be news on Margaret." She pushed the button to listen to the message.

"Ms. Powell, this is Colonel Norton. At this time we will not set up a program there in Albuquerque. Thank you for your work." The machine beeped.

Message number two. "Ms. Powell. This is Mr. Jenkins at First City National. We've considered your application for the loan to buy New Hope Ranch. Since you have no collateral, we will be unable to lend you the money at this time. If you have any questions, please call."

Sophie's legs turned to gelatin and she collapsed onto the chair.

Her eyes met Zach's. All her dreams and visions for the future evaporated in a moment of time. The glass of tea fell from her nerveless fingers.

"Oh, my." She stood and ran into the kitchen to get a

towel. She knelt over the wet place on the wooden floor and began to mop up the liquid.

Zach slipped his hand under her arm and drew her to her feet. Lifting her head, she looked at him.

"What am I going to do? I need that money. Even if the army doesn't use the ranch, what happens to the kids? And what happens to the horses?"

He pulled her against his chest, holding her.

Her brain shut down. As much as she wanted to find a way, nothing was coming.

Lord, why is this happening? I thought this was Your will.

She didn't cry and that worried Zach. He knew the devastating news set her back on her heels. He wasn't happy with what happened. There had to be a way around it.

There might not have been tears, but he felt her despair in the intensity of her hold. Her fingers dug into his back.

Resting his chin on her head, he said, "It's been a long day, Sophie. Let's go get something to eat, and afterward let's form a plan. There's been a frontal attack, so we need to counter with attack to the side or rear."

He immediately felt her body relax. She lifted her head and looked at him. "Really?"

"I've had plans go south too often while on patrol. You have to think on your feet. Let's come up with plan B. I mean, look at the success we had today. The kids were excited, their parents, your folks, my folks."

A spark of hope entered her eyes. "You're right. With

all the excitement we had this afternoon, I think we have support from the riders and their parents." She released him and stepped back. "Let me get my purse."

He ran his thumb over her cheek. "Don't give up, Sophie."

Nodding, she disappeared into her room.

Now that he had her in the fighting mode, he needed a plan. He prayed all the way to the steak place for ideas on how to deal with the problem.

As they ate their dinner, life seemed to seep back into Sophie's eyes.

"The day was a rousing success." Zach cut off a piece of steak and popped it into his mouth. "I don't think any of those riders would willingly let go of their riding time. And the volunteers wouldn't quit. Even Ollie—"

"He'd planned on retiring."

Zach shook his head in amusement. "That old boy will die in the saddle. He won't quit, but likes telling himself that he's going to walk away."

His words brought a smile to her face. "Okay, you win on that one. They'd have to take him out, toes up." Hearing her words, she stopped.

His hand closed over hers. "You didn't mean anything. I know that and if Ollie would've heard, he knows it, too."

She nodded.

An idea took shape in his mind. "I have a friend in D.C. that I could talk with to see if we could get the decision reversed." Zach told of his friend who worked at the Pentagon. He worked for a brigadier general who used to be in the cavalry unit in San Antonio. "I'd like to find out the reason why we were turned down." He had other plans, but didn't want to discuss them with her.

"So that only leaves the loan," Sophie said.

"If we could get someone to back you, someone with land or other collateral, I think the bank would lend you the money. A cosigner. You can use my town house."

She shook her head. "No, I don't—"

"Zach, oh, Zach, it is you. I told Adam it was you."

They looked up and Zach saw his ex–college girl-friend, Donna Nance. Tall and blonde, the beauty looked as if she could be a model. He stood.

"It's good to see you again," she gushed, flashing him a thousand-watt smile. "What are you doing here? The last I heard was that you lost your leg in Iraq. When I talked to some friends, they said you weren't doing so well. Surely, that can't be true, looking at you." Her gaze took him in from head to foot. "I'll just have to tell those people spreading that nonsense around they're wrong."

Each word that Donna spoke, he felt his heart close up. She made it clear when he'd been commissioned and shipped out the first time that she wasn't waiting for him. He didn't argue. "It's true, Donna. I lost my leg."

She glanced at his legs. "Oh."

Out of the corner of his eye, he saw Sophie's fingers tightening around her knife handle.

"Donna, this is Sophie Powell. She runs an equine program that helped me walk again."

"How quaint."

Sophie's eyes narrowed and the knife wavered.

Ignoring Sophie, Donna turned to him. "You're riding again? Are you going to go back to rodeo and get that championship buckle that you planned to do after you finished with the army?" Her jab hit its mark.

Silence reigned.

"You should see Zach ride," Sophie said, breaking the tension. "He's amazing to watch. He also helps others who want to ride, young kids who've lost a leg or arm. It's amazing. We always need volunteers to come and be a sidewalker for the riders. If you'd like, we'd love to have you."

Donna stiffened. "That's wonderful." She turned back to him, her smile saccharin-sweet. "I have to get back to my date. He's a real estate broker here in town, but I wanted to say hi. It's good to see you." She nodded to Sophie and air-blew a kiss to Zach.

Easing back into his chair, Zach stared down into this plate.

"Who was that?"

Zach's head came up and he saw Sophie's puzzled expression. "A friend from college."

Sophie raised a brow. "A friend?"

"A girlfriend. When I was commissioned, Donna made it clear that our relationship was over. She wasn't the waiting type, or the type to carry on a long-distance romance. She wanted to date and have fun. If I wasn't there, well, that was too bad."

Sophie didn't reply. "She wasn't worthy of you, Zach."

Her answer touched a raw spot on his soul. He didn't

want her pity. They quickly finished dinner and he drove her home.

Walking her to the door, he said, "We didn't figure out how you were going to get the money for the ranch."

"Don't worry about it, Zach. I'll think of something."

"Use my town house as collateral," he pressed again.

She shook her head. "I can't do that. Thank you for the offer." She squeezed his hand and walked inside her house.

Her refusal stung and somehow it felt connected to Donna's appearance. He didn't remember the drive to his town house but, as he sat on the couch in his living room, Donna's thoughtless words echoed in his head and heart. Who was he? Had he lost his dreams? What was he to do now?

He knew Donna was shallow, but having the homecoming queen on his arm helped his ego all those years ago. She'd stomped on that inflated ego when he left for the army. She was number one in her own eyes. He knew she wouldn't have stood by him after the accident in Iraq. But Sophie would've.

Sophie.

He remembered her reaction of her fingers clutching her knife in response to Donna's thoughtless words. Thinking back on it, he could smile at her reaction. He'd seen that protectiveness in her dealings with her clients, and he knew she'd been ready to go to bat for him. He recalled her helping Andy, trying to talk him into stroking Sam's nose or her laughing at the smile on a rider's face when they succeeded on a ride, or Sophie talking to Prince Charming about him. Even Ollie's cancer didn't stop her and she helped him in his struggle with chemotherapy.

She was a natural warrior. He would've loved to have seen her in action in Iraq. He knew she would've put everything on the line for those soldiers. And she still did.

And he knew why she fought so hard, but she didn't need to. Her brother's death wasn't her fault. Sophie's work awed him, and he prayed she'd realize that God had called her to this mission field. Wounded soldiers, whether in body or soul, needed help and he couldn't think of anyone better than Sophie. God had given her an amazing ability to work with those wounded hearts and bodies. He could vouch for that personally.

He needed her. If he was honest with himself, she'd had his heart for a long time. He'd just been too stubborn to realize it.

Her dream was in danger of not coming to fruition, but if he could do something to make it come true, he would. Picking up the phone, he called a buddy who worked in the Pentagon.

"Hey, Zach, how are you? I heard about what happened in Iraq," Dale Grant said. He and Dale had met each other the summer between his junior and senior years in college. Dale had been Reserve Officer Training Corps, or ROTC as it's known, at the University of Texas, Austin, and they'd been in the same summer maneuvers. They'd kept in touch with each other over the years.

"I'm fine. Been working hard to get back into shape by riding."

"Riding?"

Zach had the opening he wanted. "Have you heard about equine therapy?"

"I've heard something about it. Why?"

Zach launched into his speech about the benefits of horseback riding and how it made a difference in his life and attitude. "And Sophie's worked wonders with this stubborn soldier."

"So your proposal was turned down?"

"It was, but I don't know why. Could you check?"

"I'll do it."

"Dale, I've got a deadline of Friday before the owner's son needs his money or sells the property. And if you need any allies, you might call over to Walter Reed. They have a program, or connections to a program, there."

"I'm on it."

Zach next called his parents and told them of the situation. "Got any ideas?"

"I'll check with my bank to see if we can come up with the money for that ranch. What's the asking price?"

Zach gave his father the amount needed.

"I've got some resources," his father told him. "Besides, I'll call some army buddies and get something going."

"Friday's the deadline, Dad. The owner's son doesn't want Sophie to have the ranch, so he's not giving her anything beyond what his mother originally promised Sophie."

"I got it."

His mother spoke next. She had to be on the extension. "This is a lot of work to do for your sister's roommate, Zach. Is there something more your dad and I should know?"

Suddenly, Zach's mood lifted. His mother wanted to match him up with a *nice* girl and had kept after him for the last ten years.

"Mom, I'll let you know when that time comes."

"Okay. A mother can hope."

He laughed. "Dad, when you find out something, let me know."

When he hung up, he rested his head on the back of the couch. He was in love.

Love.

He stood and walked to the window, staring out into the night. What did Sophie feel? He thought she returned the feelings, but doubt haunted him. Why would she want to tie herself to a man without a leg?

Love.

Did she love him? He felt she always held something of herself back. Why? Why wouldn't she use his town house for her loan? Was she afraid to love? Did her feelings have anything to do with pity?

"Lord, I don't know what she feels, but I love her." And no matter, he'd fight for her. He might not win, but it was the right thing to do.

Chapter Fourteen

Sophie sat at the kitchen table, her Bible open, and a cup sat beside the Bible. She hadn't been able to sleep. She'd poured over Ephesians and Psalms, reading, needing some direction for hours.

Everything had fallen through. Poof. Gone.

Even Zach. She'd watched in horror last night as that awful woman made it obvious that she was shocked that Zach looked whole. Sophie watched with outrage the woman's tactless comments and Zach's retreat. Doubts had jumped him.

"What am I going to do, Lord?" she whispered. She stood and walked to the window at the end of the dining kitchen. From there, she could see the stable and the corral behind the stable.

Wasn't this the dream God gave her? Then she needed to fight for it. The odds didn't look too good for the children of Israel when they moved against Jericho. Or David against Goliath. But God didn't fail them. If He was the same yesterday, today and forever, then why would she think He would fail her now?

With a firm resolve, she walked into the bedroom to get dressed. She wasn't going to give up now.

Sophie walked down to the stables, looking for Ollie. She found him talking to Prince Charming.

"How you feeling this morning?" she asked.

He whistled. "What are you dolled up for?"

"I got a call from the bank last night. They refused the loan, but I'm going down there, see if I can talk to them and arrange another form of collateral." She shrugged. "I don't know what, but I'm going to give it my best shot. Do you feel up to running the ranch with Zach?"

"I've got some savings. I'll gladly give it to ya. These kids need this therapy. And the wounded soldiers need it, too. If my son had had this…"

Ollie's offer made her heart swell in gratitude. "Thank you, old friend, but I'm not going to do that to you. I'll get the money somehow. Will you take care of things?"

"You bet. And I know Zach will take up what I can't. Besides, all those volunteers can pitch in."

Standing on her tiptoes, she brushed a kiss on his cheek. Ollie blushed.

"Go on."

Sophie laughed and raced to her car.

Zach arrived at the ranch ten minutes after Sophie drove out. Ollie told Zach where Sophie was.

"What's she goin' do, if they don't give her the loan?" Ollie asked.

"I've called a friend I know in the Pentagon. If we can get the contract, then I think we can turn things around. But I have another idea. Every parent here, if they knew about the situation, might donate to help keep the ranch open."

Cocking his head, Ollie nodded. "I like your thinking. We're going to wrestle down that bull, no matter what."

"I'm glad we're on the same page."

Around nine-thirty, Zach's new cell phone rang. He'd gotten the thing the day of graduation and knew he needed to give his parents and Sophie the number, but with all that had happened, it had slipped his mind. Pulling it out of his shirt pocket, he noted the call was his friend in D.C.

"Hey, Dale, you've got news for me?" Zach asked.

"I need you to fly to D.C., Zach, ASAP. I've got a couple of people we need to see. Can you get here by five this afternoon?"

"I can. I'll see you then." Closing the phone, Zach looked up and saw Ollie. "You heard?"

"Some."

"I've got to fly to Washington to talk to the powers that be. We've got a shot."

"Go."

"If you call Beth and Ethan, they can make the rest of the calls to the parents." Zach reached into his pocket and pulled out a tablet. "Let me give you their numbers. And my new cell-phone number. You show that to Sophie when you see her."

Ollie took the paper and darted into the tack room for a pencil and scribbled the numbers down. "Don't worry. I've got it in hand."

Zach grinned. "We're going to do this." He took off, his mission clear.

Sophie sat in her car outside the bank. The loan officer was sympathetic but he wasn't going to give her the loan. No army contract, no money.

She rested her forehead on the steering wheel. Now what? An outrageous idea popped into her head, startling her. But the more she thought about it, the more the idea appealed to her. She started her car and headed south. Her hometown of Tijeras was southwest of the city, about a forty-five-minute drive.

She prayed every mile she drove for wisdom and the words to say to her parents.

Tijeras had changed. There was a new gas station/convenience store just inside the city limits. Also a new fast-food fried-chicken restaurant stood across the street from the gas station. Down two blocks on Main Street a new Mexican food restaurant occupied the corner where McFarley's Ice Cream shop had stood.

Sophie turned down a side street, Locust, and pulled up to her parents' house. Her father had painted the porch. The cactus in the front yard had grown and sage bushes dotted the rocks and dirt in the yard. She pulled into the driveway. Her father's car stood outside the garage. He worked out of his home office. He was the insurance salesman/adjuster for several counties. She walked up to the side door. It stood open, but the screen door was locked. Music floated outside.

She knocked.

Her mother appeared, dressed in jeans and a paint-splattered smock over her T-shirt.

"Hi, Mom."

Cindy stood frozen for a moment.

"Can I come in?"

The words broke into her fog. "Sure." She moved to the door and unlatched the hook from the eye.

Sophie climbed the two steps to the door and walked inside.

"What are you doing here?" Cindy asked.

It wasn't a good beginning. Sophie knew she could make chitchat, but she'd never done small talk with her mother, was never ever able to tell her mother about her school days or about having a boyfriend, or going to her high school prom. "I need your help."

"Jim," her mother called out. "Come to the kitchen." While they waited for her father, Cindy asked, "You want some coffee?"

"No thanks, Mom."

Her father appeared in the doorway. "Sophie, what are you doing here?"

"I wanted to talk to you and Mom about the ranch. The bank won't give me a loan to buy the place." She explained the situation. "I know you have that big parcel of land just outside of Santa Fe. I know you want to build on it, but I was hoping maybe to use it as collateral for the loan."

Her parents looked at her as if she were speaking Chinese.

Suddenly, her mother stood, the chair tipping back and falling to the floor.

"How dare you. You know how I feel about horses and you want us to throw away our retirement on a horse ranch? No."

"Now, Cindy—" her father began.

Turning on him, she yelled, "Don't 'now, Cindy' me. How could you even think I'd want to have anything to do with horses after what happened?" She rounded on Sophie. "I don't know why you thought we'd give you money for that."

Sophie stood. "The ranch helps a lot of people overcome handicaps. I know it's what I'm to do."

"And you don't care about my feelings?" Cindy demanded.

Sophie glanced at her father. He sat there, immobile. There was no hope here. "I'm sorry I asked," Sophie said.

She turned to go.

"You should've known," her mother cried.

Pausing at the door, Sophie glanced over her shoulder. "You're right. I should've known, but I thought after so many years…" She shrugged. "I'm sorry, Mom, that it wasn't me who died that day. I've regretted my actions every moment since then. And there's not been a moment when I haven't tried to make up for it. But Zach finally made me see that Matt's death was an accident. I pray you can see that, too." She pushed open the door and walked to her car.

Numbness settled on Sophie until she reached her grandmother's house on the opposite side of town. She sat in her car, frozen, until her grandmother noticed her in the car. The older woman coaxed her inside and sat her on the sofa. After several questions, Sophie told her what had just happened with her mother.

"I thought, Grandma, if I tried hard enough maybe Mom would love me. And maybe Dad would speak up for me. If I tried to save others, give my life to make up for what I did, maybe—" She shook her head. "I was wrong."

Her grandmother wrapped her arms around Sophie. "I love you, child. And I think your mother loves you in her own way. It was easier for her to live in her grief than go on. I was never so proud as I was when I saw those kids riding yesterday." Her grandmother cupped Sophie's face. "It's going to be okay."

Sophie laid her head on her grandmother's shoulder and tried to shut out the pain.

When Sophie pulled into the parking lot of the ranch, she saw an ambulance by the stable. Quickly parking, she ran to the ambulance. She saw an unconscious Ollie on the gurney.

"What happened?"

The paramedic turned to her. "He was found unconscious on the floor. Are you related to him?"

"No, but he's a longtime employee and friend. He's on chemo for cancer."

The paramedic nodded. "Thanks for the heads-up." He climbed in the back and started to close the door.

"What hospital?"

"ABQ General." He closed the door and the ambulance took off.

Sophie looked around at the volunteers. "Anyone know what happened?"

One of the teen volunteers said, "I walked into the stable and found him on the floor by the tack room. When I couldn't wake him, I called 911."

Scanning the crowd, Sophie asked, "Where's Zach?"

"You know, I haven't seen him, but I got here about three."

"Has anyone seen Zach?" Sophie scanned the faces of the volunteers, but no one had seen him.

"Let me change and let's cancel all lessons and feed the horses."

The five volunteers standing in the parking lot scattered.

Sophie raced into her house. As she changed she wondered where Zach was and what had happened.

The doors to ICU closed. She walked into the waiting room for another chance to hold Ollie's hand for five minutes in the next hour. He looked old and frail, not like the hard-as-nails foreman she knew.

She dialed Zach's home phone number, but only got his answering machine. She called Beth. "Have you heard from your brother?"

"Zach? No. Why?"

"He's vanished. He wasn't at the ranch today, and he's not in his apartment. Did he ever get a cell phone like we begged him? I know he said he would, but I haven't heard anything."

"He talked about getting one, but I don't know if he did. He hasn't called me, so I don't know where he is. Call my parents. They might know."

"Is there—"

"I've got to go, friend. That's the last call for my plane."

The phone went dead.

Sophie stared at the useless instrument. She wasn't going to call Zach's parents. She'd sound like a desperate woman. Maybe he didn't want to hear from her after meeting his ex-girlfriend last night.

Lord, I thought he'd healed. Was I wrong? What's happened? They're all gone. Zach, Ollie, my parents, Margaret. There's no one.

Despair overwhelmed her. After she saw Ollie one more time, held his hand and prayed, she drove home. Her heart led her to the stable. Horses had always been a comfort for her. She found Prince Charming in his stall. He bobbed his head, greeting her. In the corner, opposite the stall, rested a cane. Zach's cane, which he kept here for times when he was exhausted and his leg was bothering him.

Resting her head on Prince Charming's dark neck, the fear and despair overwhelmed her.

"Oh, Prince Charming, what am I going to do? It's all vanished overnight."

Prince Charming stood quietly. Well, at least she had her horses for now.

And God was there in the silence and grief.

* * *

Sophie woke up and looked around her. The morning light streamed through the crack in the walls of the stall. Straw under her hands and a saddle blanket under her cheek confused her. Prince Charming nosed her.

Prince Charming? Straw?

Suddenly the memories flooded back. She'd fallen asleep in Prince Charming's stall. He nosed her again.

"Thanks for the wake-up call, boy," she said climbing to her feet. She picked straw out of her hair. Letting herself out of the stall, she walked to the office and splashed water on her face. Looking into the mirror, she saw the circles under her eyes.

She moved out of the bathroom and grabbed the phone. She called the hospital, asking for Intensive Care. Sophie discovered that Ollie had awakened and been moved to a private room.

"Thank You, Lord," she whispered, hanging up the phone.

She needed to rush up to the house, change and snatch an apple before she started with the horses. Racing back to Prince Charming's stall, she grabbed her purse and started toward the house.

The sound of tires on the gravel drew her attention to the road. Zach's truck drove up. He stopped by her car and he got out, but there was another passenger in the front seat. The stranger opened the passenger door and joined Zach beside the car. Whoever he was, he was an army major.

"I've got good news for you, Sophie," Zach began.

"So you decided to show up?"

"What are you talking about?"

"Where were you yesterday? Ollie's in the hospital. When I came home, I found the paramedics loading him into an ambulance and all the volunteers shaken up, telling me how they found him."

Zach's face lost its color. "How is he?"

"He's out of intensive care. The hospital is optimistic."

Out of the corner of her eye, she saw the major who watched her outburst.

"This is Major Dale Grant. I was in Washington yesterday, trying to get approval for us to run a program here." Zach ran his fingers through his hair. "Dale and I wanted you to know the good news. We got the contract. He also wanted to see the ranch for himself after hearing my glowing reviews. He and I go back a long way. He's also a horseman."

She stood there frozen, feeling overjoyed and excited that their dream was coming true. And—stupid. Stupid and petty for her comments.

The major stepped close, offering his hand.

She shook it, her face blazing with color. "I'm sorry, sir, for my outburst. My only excuse is it's been a terrible thirty-six hours." She glanced at Zach, her heart in her throat. "I couldn't get the loan, so your efforts might be in vain."

Before he could respond, another car drove up. It was her father's car. What was happening? Sophie wondered. Much to her amazement, her parents stepped out of the front seat, and her grandmother out of the backseat.

Cindy McClure walked up to Sophie. Her mother

smiled, but her lips trembled. "After you left yesterday, I thought about what you said. I never wanted you to die instead of your brother. Forgive me."

Sophie couldn't believe her ears. She wondered if she was still asleep in Prince Charming's stall.

Cindy glanced at her mother. "When Mom came to the house yesterday, we decided that there have been too many times when hurt feelings have kept us apart. And we also decided to put that property up for you as collateral. Your father called his banker last night and we were given the loan."

Tears silently flowed down Sophie's cheeks. "Oh, Mother." Sophie slipped into her mother's arms. She felt her father wrap his arms around both of them. The wall surrounding her heart just shattered. The love and approval she'd longed for from her parents was just given.

After a moment, Jim released them and Sophie turned to the major. "It looks like that program will be implemented." She glanced at Zach. He stood there watching. There was something in his eyes that told her of his feelings. She wanted to ask him—

Before she could say anything, more cars drove into the parking lot—a half dozen to a dozen. Doors slammed, and Beth appeared among the parents and kids who were part of the therapy program. Excitement raced through the air.

Andy's mom appeared. She looked around, then turned back to Sophie. "Yesterday Zach told me about what happened."

She glanced over her shoulder to where Zach stood.

He shrugged his shoulders and smiled as if to say, you should have trusted me.

Andy's mom continued, "I told him I wanted to help, so he and I called a lot of people. I told my church and we collected money. All the other students and parents gave, too. We've collected close to five thousand dollars for you to use as a down payment on the ranch." She handed Sophie a check.

Sophie's hands shook as she looked down at the check. She felt Zach move beside her.

"You have a lot of grateful parents."

She nodded through her tears.

A tug on her jeans brought her gaze down.

"I helped, too," Andy added. "I stacked the money." His chest puffed out.

"Thank you." She turned to the crowd, fighting the tears and overwhelmed with gratitude. "I want to thank everyone for your generous hearts. This tells me that this ranch is as important to you as it is to me."

"We love you, Miss Sophie," Andy called out.

Everyone clapped.

Another car drove up and parked. Austin Stillwell got out. The crowd quieted.

Austin walked to where Sophie stood. "We need to talk."

Before Sophie could respond, Zach said, "I think whatever you have to say to Sophie you can say in front of her family and the people she serves."

Zach stepped closer and Sophie took courage from his presence.

Austin's mouth flattened with rage. His eyes narrowed as he focused on Sophie. "Do you have my money?"

"I do. We can go to the bank and have the check cut. Name the time."

He didn't look happy. "One o'clock this afternoon at First National." He whirled and strode to his car.

As he drove off, boos and hisses followed him.

Sophie turned to the crowd. "Thank you for all your work. Your support means so much to me. For today, lessons are cancelled."

Laughter filled the air.

Before the crowd could disperse, Zach raised his hands. "Wait."

People stopped and turned back to him and Sophie. No one said a word.

Zach offered up a prayer for wisdom. Last night, once they got the approval, Zach knew what he wanted to do the instant he got back home. Sophie's initial reaction threw him, dampening his hopes for their future. But he knew he had to gamble, take the risk of showing his heart to her. He had to take a leap of faith. He'd planned on talking to her in private, but something told him *now* was the right time and place,

Zach caught Sophie's hands. "I want to tell you what an amazing woman you are. Your vision has set me on the right road, but it's also become my vision. This is what I want to do to show others how to overcome whatever life throws at them. You have a strength and courage that awes and humbles me. You saw me as the man God wanted me to be and I want to be involved with this therapy program—"

She opened her mouth to respond, but his finger came up and he lightly pressed it to her lips.

"The position I want, Sophie, is as your husband. I love you and have loved you since I stomped into my parents' kitchen wet and disgruntled all those years ago. You took my breath away and still do. I hope you'll take pity on this beat-up cowboy and say yes. I've found my true purpose in this life and my true love."

Not a sound came from the gathered crowd.

"What do you say, Miss Sophie?" Andy asked, breaking the silence. "I like him. Besides, he's got a neat leg that makes him special."

The crowd laughed.

"He's right. I do have that extraspecial leg," Zach whispered.

Joy welled up in her eyes and her smile reflected it. "Yes."

The cheers surrounded them, but her eyes never left Zach's face. Pulling her into his arms, he sealed the deal with a kiss.

Epilogue

Sun filtered through the windows as Sophie sat at the kitchen table. Her mother and grandmother fussed over her hair, putting yellow and white daisies into the curls pinned on the back of her head. Her father stood on the porch, talking to Ollie. The last two weeks were like a dream—she'd talked with her parents, telling them all about the things in her heart, her dreams, her time in college and Iraq. Both her father and mother had listened and questioned her about a dozen different things. And they made sure she knew how proud they were of her. They even shared memories of Matt.

Both her parents had come to the ranch and trained to be sidewalkers. She'd even seen her mother smile at one of the little girls who had Down's. Molly adored her mother. Her mother blossomed giving to others. Sophie discovered her mother's marvelous talent for organization, taking the volunteer lists and perfecting a new schedule. Her father helped with the veterans. They had two soldiers in the program and would get another couple next week. Her grandma had accompanied her mother several times and worked in the office.

Zach's parents also visited frequently, helped with chores and started training another horse to be used by the soldiers.

"That's it," her mother declared, patting Sophie on the shoulder. "You look wonderful."

Sophie looked down at the white lace top and white tiered Western skirt and turquoise-and-coral Western belt. Her new boots had an edge of turquoise around the tops and the tips of the boot. She stood and hugged her mother. "I'm glad you're here."

"I'm glad, too," Cindy whispered.

Her grandmother beamed at Sophie over Cindy's shoulder.

Her dad opened the front door. "You ladies ready?" he called.

"We are."

When Sophie appeared on the porch, only her father stood there. He offered his arm. Her mother and grand-mother walked ahead of them.

People filled the bleachers and spilled out between the rings and the shade trees beyond. Tables stood behind the group, filled with a wedding cake, buñue-los, fruits and punch. She saw Zach standing under the trees, Ethan and Prince Charming with a silver-concha studded halter beside him.

Zach. He looked like her dream in a white Western shirt, starched jeans and boots.

Sophie and her father stopped at the entrance to the stable. Beth held Sam's reins, daisies and pink cornflowers woven into her halter. Beth handed Sophie her bouquet, which was composed of the same flowers and flowing ribbons.

"You ready for this?" Beth teased. "You ready to hitch yourself to that ornery brother of mine?"

Sophie looked at her intended. "I've been ready for this since I saw him standing in your parents' kitchen, mad as all get-out that he'd ruined his new boots."

Beth laughed. She led Sam out into the sunlight. She stopped by Andy. "You ready for your part?"

"Yes."

Guitars began the wedding march.

Andy proudly walked down to Zach, waving at his mother and friends in the audience. Zach pulled the young man to his side. Prince Charming nudged Zach on the shoulder. Zach glanced at the horse, then his brother. Ethan laughed.

Beth walked down the path, leading Sam. The gathered crowd rose as Sophie and her father walked to Zach and the preacher.

Zach's heart skipped a beat when Sophie came into view. The sunlight danced off her hair, giving her a heavenly look. She was so beautiful, inside and out. He never would've imagined the changes to his life, and never would've thought of this turn. *Lord, thank You. She is a woman of great virtue.*

He didn't know how he'd been blessed with her. Out of horror came joy and hope.

Sophie stopped beside him. Her feelings of joy and gratefulness were clearly reflected in her eyes. He returned her sentiments. Her father kissed Sophie's cheek, gave her hand to Zach and stepped back.

Zach squeezed her hand and she squeezed back, sealing their joy.

The preacher—their preacher—opened his Bible, and a butterfly landed on the daisy in Sophie's hair. The photographer captured the picture.

"I think we've been sent a blessing from above," Zach murmured.

"Amen," Sophie answered.

* * * * *

Dear Reader,

When I read in our local newspaper about an equine therapy ranch in the area, I was hooked. They worked with children, but wanted to work with wounded veterans. Since then, I learned about NARAH and their national website (www.narha.org/Horses%20For%20 Heroes/NARHAHorsesforHeroes.asp).

On their website I found an article about how horses are being used to help the wounded veterans. "I Will Never Leave a Fallen Comrade" was the title of an article from the 2006 Fall edition of *Narah's Stories*. The work they do is amazing and inspiring.

Both Sophie and Zach are ex-soldiers who love horses. They are two wounded souls who have to learn how to trust God again when the plans for their lives have been blown up. It is a journey of faith. It is a journey of hope. I pray you enjoyed their journey.

Leann Harris

QUESTIONS FOR DISCUSSION

1. When we first meet Zach, he has yet to deal with the reality of his life. Do you think his actions were justified?

2. Do you think Sophie's tough-love approach to Zach was the right way to go? What about how his parents dealt with him?

3. Ever had a time when you didn't know how to handle the situation like Zach's parents? What did you do when you felt helpless?

4. Was Sophie's reaction to Zach's interest in her valid? Do you think her doubting his feelings were justified?

5. When Sophie brought the light saber to the exercise ring, were you surprised? Have you heard of the unit in the army that is old-fashioned cavalry?

6. Have you ever doubted the direction of your life as both Sophie and Zach did? How did you deal with it?

7. Was Ollie's desire to keep his illness from Sophie the right thing to do? Should he have leveled with her?

8. Margaret's son was jealous of Sophie's relationship with his mother. Why do you think he felt that way? Was it reasonable?

9. Were you surprised with how much equine therapy is used? Is it a smart thing to do?

10. Sophie overheard her parents' grieving over her brother's death. She thought they blamed her. She blamed herself. Was her reaction over-the-top? Was she justified in her feelings?

11. What did you think of Sophie's mother's handling of her son's death? Her father? Have you known a relative or friend who got stuck over an incident and can't go beyond that? How did you handle that?

12. How do you feel about Sophie's refusal to use Zach's town house for collateral?

13. Were you surprised by Sophie's parents' reaction to her asking for the collateral to buy the ranch?

14. What was your reaction to Zach's meeting his old girlfriend and her reaction to seeing him?

15. What do you think of Zach's solution to the bank's refusal to give Sophie the loan?

TITLES AVAILABLE NEXT MONTH

Available January 25, 2011

CHILD OF GRACE
Irene Hannon

THE PRODIGAL COMES HOME
Mirror Lake
Kathryn Springer

HOMETOWN DAD
Kellerville
Merrillee Whren

SEASON OF DREAMS
Jenna Mindel

HER VALENTINE FAMILY
Renee Andrews

SECOND CHANCE COURTSHIP
Glynna Kaye

REQUEST YOUR FREE BOOKS!

2 FREE INSPIRATIONAL NOVELS
PLUS 2
FREE
MYSTERY GIFTS

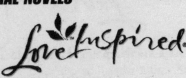

YES! Please send me 2 FREE Love Inspired® novels and my 2 FREE mystery gifts (gifts are worth about $10). After receiving them, if I don't wish to receive any more books, I can return the shipping statement marked "cancel." If I don't cancel, I will receive 6 brand-new novels every month and be billed just $4.24 per book in the U.S. or $4.74 per book in Canada. That's a saving of over 20% off the cover price. It's quite a bargain! Shipping and handling is just 50¢ per book.* I understand that accepting the 2 free books and gifts places me under no obligation to buy anything. I can always return a shipment and cancel at any time. Even if I never buy another book, the two free books and gifts are mine to keep forever.

105/305 IDN E7PP

Name	(PLEASE PRINT)

Address	Apt. #

City	State/Prov.	Zip/Postal Code

Signature (if under 18, a parent or guardian must sign)

Mail to Steeple Hill Reader Service:
IN U.S.A.: P.O. Box 1867, Buffalo, NY 14240-1867
IN CANADA: P.O. Box 609, Fort Erie, Ontario L2A 5X3

Not valid for current subscribers to Love Inspired books.

Want to try two free books from another series?
Call 1-800-873-8635 or visit www.morefreebooks.com.

* Terms and prices subject to change without notice. Prices do not include applicable taxes. N.Y. residents add applicable sales tax. Canadian residents will be charged applicable provincial taxes and GST. Offer not valid in Quebec. This offer is limited to one order per household. All orders subject to approval. Credit or debit balances in a customer's account(s) may be offset by any other outstanding balance owed by or to the customer. Please allow 4 to 6 weeks for delivery. Offer available while quantities last.

Your Privacy: Steeple Hill Books is committed to protecting your privacy. Our Privacy Policy is available online at www.SteepleHill.com or upon request from the Reader Service. From time to time we make our lists of customers available to reputable third parties who may have a product or service of interest to you. If you would prefer we not share your name and address, please check here. ☐

Help us get it right—We strive for accurate, respectful and relevant communications. To clarify or modify your communication preferences, visit us at www.ReaderService.com/consumerschoice.

LIREG10R

Enjoy a sneak peek at Valerie Hansen's adventurous historical-romance novel RESCUING THE HEIRESS, available February, only from Love Inspired Historical

"I think your profession is most honorable."

One more quick glance showed him that Tess was smiling, and it was all he could do to keep from breaking into a face-splitting grin at her praise. There was something impish yet charming about the banker's daughter. Always had been, if he were totally honest with himself.

Someday, Michael vowed silently, he would find a suitable woman with a spirit like Tess's and give her a proper courting. He had no chance with Tess herself, of course. That went without saying. Still, she couldn't be the only appealing lass in San Francisco. Besides, most men waited to wed until they could properly look after a wife and family.

If he'd been a rich man's son instead of the offspring of a lowly sailor, however, perhaps he'd have shown a personal interest in Miss Clark or one of her socialite friends already.

Would he really have? he asked himself. He doubted it. There was a part of Michael that was repelled by the affectations of the wealthy, by the way they lorded it over the likes of him and his widowed mother. He knew Tess couldn't help that she'd been born into a life of luxury, yet he still found her background off-putting.

Which is just as well, he reminded himself. It was bad enough that they were likely to be seen out and about on this particular evening. If the maid Annie Dugan hadn't been along as a chaperone, he knew their time together could, if misinterpreted, lead to his ruination. His career with the fire department depended upon a sterling reputation as well as a

Spartan lifestyle and strong work ethic.

Michael had labored too long and hard to let anything spoil his pending promotion to captain. He set his jaw and grasped the reins of the carriage more tightly. Not even the prettiest, smartest, most persuasive girl in San Francisco was going to get away with doing that.

He sighed, realizing that Miss Tess Clark fit that description to a T.

You won't be able to put down the rest of
Tess and Michael's romantic love story,
available in February 2011,
only from Love Inspired Historical.

Love Inspired
HISTORICAL

INSPIRATIONAL HISTORICAL ROMANCE

Dr. Ben Drake has always held a special place in his heart for strays. The ultimate test of his compassion comes when the fragile beauty at his door is revealed to be his brother's widow. Callie could expose the Drakes' darkest family secrets but just one look at her and Ben knows he can't turn her away—not when he can lead her to true love and God's forgiving grace.

Rocky Mountain Redemption

by
PAMELA NISSEN

*Available February
wherever books are sold.*

Steeple
Hill®

LIH82857

Love Inspired

SUSPENSE

RIVETING INSPIRATIONAL ROMANCE

TEXAS RANGER JUSTICE

Keeping the Lone Star State safe

Follow the men and women of the Texas Rangers,
as they risk their lives to help save others,
with

DAUGHTER OF TEXAS by **Terri Reed**
January 2011

BODY OF EVIDENCE by **Lenora Worth**
February 2011

FACE OF DANGER by **Valerie Hansen**
March 2011

TRAIL OF LIES by **Margaret Daley**
April 2011

THREAT OF EXPOSURE by **Lynette Eason**
May 2011

OUT OF TIME by **Shirlee McCoy**
June 2011

Available wherever books are sold.

www.SteepleHill.com

Steeple
Hill®

LISCONT11